*"A woman alone\
You think it's saf*

"It looked like you took a pretty bad spill," Kyle went on.

Gillian didn't reply at once. Here was Kyle Dayton standing before her, looking handsome and concerned and solid, and she wanted so desperately to rush into his arms and say, "It's been so long since anyone has really and truly cared about me...."

Instead, she settled for "Sure, it's safe out here," accompanied by a self-confident smile. "Anyway, like I said earlier, I'm a tough city girl."

"Regular roller-derby material." He returned her smile.

She hated that. His smiles weakened her. And the idea that he might be able to see past her carefully boarded shutters smacked dangerously of intimacy. The territory was already far too treacherous. There was moonlight and water and soft earth to lie upon. There was a man and a woman....

Dear Reader,

Welcome to the Silhouette **Special Edition**
experience! With your search for consistently
satisfying reading in mind, every month the authors
and editors of Silhouette **Special Edition** aim to offer
you a stimulating blend of deep emotions and high
romance.

The name Silhouette **Special Edition** and the
distinctive arch on the cover represent a
commitment—a commitment to bring you six
sensitive, substantial novels each month. In the
pages of a Silhouette **Special Edition**, compelling
true-to-life characters face riveting emotional
issues—and come out winners. Both celebrated
authors and newcomers to the series strive for depth
and dimension, vividness and warmth, in writing
these stories of living and loving in today's world.

The result, we hope, is romance you can believe in.
Deeply emotional, richly romantic, infinitely
rewarding—that's the Silhouette **Special Edition**
experience. Come share it with us—six times a
month!

From all the authors and editors of Silhouette
Special Edition,

Best wishes,

Leslie Kazanjian,
Senior Editor

JENNIFER WEST
Last Stand

Silhouette Special Edition

Published by Silhouette Books New York

America's Publisher of Contemporary Romance

SILHOUETTE BOOKS
300 East 42nd St., New York, N.Y. 10017

ISBN: 0-373-09552-X

First Silhouette Books printing September 1989

Printed in the U.S.A.

Books by Jennifer West

Silhouette Intimate Moments

A Season of Rainbows #10
Star Spangled Days #31
Edge of Venus #71
Main Chance #99

Silhouette Special Edition

Earth and Fire #262
Return to Paradise #283
Moments of Glory #339
Object of Desire #366
Come Pride, Come Passion #383
Sometimes a Miracle #404
Greek to Me #432
Tender Is the Knight #476
Last Stand #552

JENNIFER WEST's

first career was in musical comedy, as a professional singer and dancer. She turned her love for drama to the printed page, where she now gets to play all the parts—and direct the action. She lives in Southern California but travels frequently in search of adventures—and sometimes misadventures!—to share with her readers.

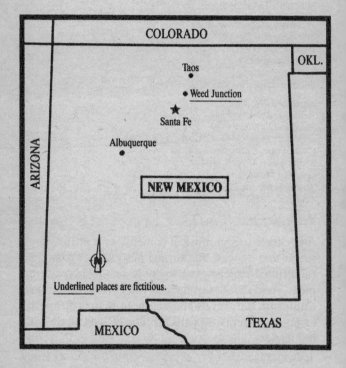

COLORADO

OKL.

• Taos

• Weed Junction

★
Santa Fe

Albuquerque
•

NEW MEXICO

ARIZONA

Underlined places are fictitious.

MEXICO

TEXAS

Chapter One

Outside, the church bell pealed with abrupt, raucous energy.

Gillian McGuire looked up from her half-packed suitcase. In the three weeks she had been there, she had come to know Weed Junction's moods and schedules. Something was up...because something was off. The assault on the afternoon silence did not fit the usual lethargic ebb and flow of the town's life.

She left her place by the bed and walked barefoot to the hotel room's only window. Pushing aside a slatted wooden shutter, she peered down the parched earthen street to where the New Mexico sun beat against the church of San Geronimo. Still, there wasn't anything interesting to see.

Lifting her hair off her shoulders, she twisted the heavy fall of brown curls into a tight bun, and held it in place on top of her head while she drew in a dry, hot breath. The air tasted of sage and dust, and for a brief instant she felt a bittersweet connection with her surroundings. Long after she was gone, something of herself would always remain there.

Gillian's gaze took in San Geronimo's shining white bell tower. She did not believe in Indian legends, timetables put out by airlines, or the vows people exchanged when they slipped on wedding bands. Still, seeing San Geronimo as it presently appeared, glowing with the curious, otherworldly light of the region, she was almost tempted to buy the local mythology that claimed Indian gods resided within its confines as roommates of the Christian God.

She had almost succumbed to the haunted beauty of the land, imagining rocks had eyes and trees arms, wishing in a way that the Indian legends of shape-changers might be real, so that the owl that flew before the moon was a wise man and the cat that called on a ridge could in its kindness lift her from her own life's despair.

Among locals, these stories of gods and miracles and strange occurrences grew particularly florid in the Kachina Kantina across the way. For a time, Gillian had even kept a notebook of the folklore, grandiosely thinking of herself as a future female Castaneda.

She saw a series of books, her name emblazoned on the covers. Inside the book jacket it would say: *Gillian McGuire, noted along with Margaret Mead as being one of the foremost cultural anthropologists, has added to the world's storehouse of knowledge by...*

Of course, her flights of fancy only proved to be as optimistically delusional as her marriage had been. But so what? After all, she *had* made *some* progress.

She shifted her gaze to the Kachina Kantina. It had taken her six long years to discover what a miserable cad Scott was, but only three days to figure out that the only spirits in Weed Junction were contained in bottles behind the bar.

The bell had not let up its urgent clamor, and Gillian looked back to the arched courtyard entrance, then beyond to the chapel proper and higher, where she could see John Proudfeather in the open tower.

In shadow, his body swayed vigorously back and forth as he pulled on the rope. There were the familiar flash of red from his shirt and a fleeting glimpse of yellow and blue headband as he leaned into view, then quickly disappeared behind the bell.

Gillian squinted. John Proudfeather's sudden animation was, in itself, perplexing. Eighty-six years old and lazy as a rock, Proudfeather would additionally feign hearing and sight impairment when it suited him. Gillian knew enough about human nature to understand that it was his character and not his advanced age that accounted for both sloth and deception. She also suspected—having had her own dealings with the Indian—that he was as clever as a fox.

The notes continued to rise over the town. Maybe, Gillian thought, this was about a wedding.

In that case, she was glad to be missing it. Since Scott, weddings had lost their charm.

At the thought of Scott a gloom descended over her. But before the useless, senseless tears could come again, she turned her mind to the future.

In fifteen minutes she would be heading out, suitcase packed, to put her life back together.

And if some fools were getting married...well, that was one funeral she wasn't going to be around to attend.

Kyle Dayton pushed the brim of his Stetson lower over his forehead, then cupped his eyes against the sun's glare and squinted down the dirt road in both directions, searching for signs of life. At the same time, his ears were tuned for the friendly hum of another vehicle.

But the air only rang with an overpowering silence.

A spell of utter loneliness seemed to have been cast upon the land. Not even the dark silhouette of a bird broke the blue expanse of sky that stretched over the valley between the Taos Mountains in the Sangre de Cristo and Brazos ranges. Kyle had read about the area, had seen photographs, had even listened to others wax poetic about this region's light and the awesome beauty that could rearrange a man's soul; but nothing had prepared him for the grandeur now surrounding him.

To the Indians this land was sacred. Magic lived in the harsh landscape—or so said the tourist brochures. Death, too, resided in this territory. A person didn't need a pamphlet to be clear on that.

Near him at the side of the road, the new blue GMC pickup truck rented in Albuquerque had long since stopped its fizzing. It had been only twenty minutes since the vehicle had clunked to a halt, but already Kyle's mind was conjuring up three-dimensional shapes of cold beer cans.

At first he had thought to wait in the cab of the truck, thinking it would only be minutes before a passing motorist would happen by with an offer of help. But that had been naively optimistic. The New Mexico desert wasn't L.A. with a car whizzing by every two seconds, and the truck had turned rapidly into an inhospitable environment. In the end it had been better to stand outside.

Around him the wilderness extended forever. On the other side of the road, a green blanket of sage stretched like a river, spilling from distant high mountains cast in pink and red and salmon by the bold light.

But nowhere was there the comforting sign of other humanity.

Something would turn up, he assured himself with bravado as he set off down the road.

Spirals of fine dust rose in his wake. It was so quiet that he imagined he could hear the minuscule particles of earth fall and settle into place again. Each step proved to be an effort; the formerly comfortable Tony Lama boots had become burning lead weights on his feet.

What irony if after everything he died like this— withered and dehydrated in a desert. In spite of his physical discomfort, his lips curled into a half smile as he thought how horribly perfect that would be: a fitting ending worthy of Hollywood. The double twist.

A year ago, at the peak of his career, he had faced the specter of death—cancer. But like one of the heroes he had played so often on the wide silver screen, he had vanquished his oppressor. And now, as he strode fit in body and with his mind finally directed toward the most meaningful goal of his life, he would fall—a casualty of a busted radiator. It was unglamorous. It was real.

Kyle's smile broadened. He visualized the scenario that would follow his demise. *People* would do a cover-story retrospective on his life. There'd be lots of lies, plenty of gossip, the requisite two or three days of hysteria, during which time a lot of people would weep, just as they had over James Dean and Marilyn Monroe. Certainly his agent and business manager would mourn their percentages. And Gordon Millman, whom Kyle had walked out on—forfeiting an acting contract worth three million dollars in order to follow his own dream—would dance on his grave.

It was then that Kyle heard the bell.

At first he thought the heat was getting to him. Earlier, the radio had given the day's temperature as one hundred four degrees. So that was it; his brain was boiling and dementia was setting in. Soon the buzzards would circle.

But no....

Kyle stopped and listened.

It was a real bell, a church bell. Taking heart, he strained to determine from which direction the sounds came, then set off again with hope in his heart and the vision of a cold beer in his mind.

Gillian lugged her suitcase down to the lobby, then made four more trips back up the stairs to get the boxes of research books, notebooks and paper, plus her portable typewriter.

When all her worldly belongings were removed from above, she knocked loudly on the hotel office door.

Inside the room Spanish music was blaring. Gillian could hear Stella Sanchez's voice rise and fall with passionate intensity as she sang along with the record.

"Stella!" Gillian shouted over the music. "Stella . . . I'm going!"

The music stopped. "Hey?"

"It's me—Gillian. I'm taking off now." Gillian heard the sharp rap of Stella's high heels as she moved across the room. The thick, arched door creaked open, and Stella Sanchez appeared. She was dressed in a tight Hawaiian print dress. Her dark hair was brushed to one side, reminding Gillian of Hedy Lamarr. Over the other ear, Stella had inserted a large, saucy red paper flower. Fashion excess was a passion with her. No matter what the time of day, Stella was always dressed in something vivid, as if, Gillian supposed, she thought she was in some town other than Weed Junction.

"So," Stella said, "you're going to leave." It was an accusation more than an implied question.

Gillian nodded. "Yup."

"You give up too easy. Not me. If I want something, I never give up." Stella tossed her head, a dramatic gesture she employed often when she expounded on her attributes. "Someday I'm gonna be a singer in Vegas. It'll happen, just wait," she insisted, as if Gillian had contradicted her.

Abruptly Stella's attention shifted. She studied Gillian for an instant, then shook her head, closed her dark eyes momentarily, and sighing morosely, said, "You know, you'd have a man if you dressed yourself up a little bit."

"I don't want a man," said Gillian. Her tone held conviction. They had had this same conversation at least fifty times during the last three weeks.

Gillian knew very well how she looked. And didn't care—at least not lately.

At the present time she was wearing one of her favorite outfits: it was comfortable and colorful, even— she thought—marginally cheerful. But most of all it was cool. A pair of blue denim cutoff jeans, a yellow T-shirt, cropped to a couple of inches below her breasts, a pair of natural leather sandals that she had bought in Mexico, and a beaded Indian headband given to her by John Proudfeather, with the confession that it had been made in Taiwan.

"You've got to want a man," insisted Stella, never one to change course once she had set off in a direction. "Every normal woman wants a man."

"I had a man. It was a miserable experience."

Stella shrugged and hitched up her strapless dress. Her abundant bosom jiggled provocatively, the way it did whenever Stella took herself over to the Kachina Kantina and paraded around for the cowboys and locals. Sometimes, after a few tequilas, she would hop onto a table and sing along with the jukebox as if she were on a spotlighted stage. "Yeah," Stella said. "Men. I don't know that I like them much myself. But still . . . what else is there?"

Gillian returned to the business at hand. "I stopped by for the receipt."

Stella blinked, then remembered. "Oh, yeah. It's ready." Her attention drifted to the suitcase and Gillian's four cardboard boxes, the sight rooting her to the spot. "That's it? I thought you had more stuff up there," Stella said.

"Nope. This is all I came with." *This is all I have,* Gillian qualified to herself.

"Well, anyway, you used to have a house and stuff, huh?" Stella said, pivoting on her narrow high heels and going back into her apartment, which served both as office and residence.

Gillian waited in the lobby by the open door. "Yes, a house."

"A big one?"

"Not big."

"But nice."

"Yes. It was nice." A vision of the house began to form in her mind, starting as a faint outline. Gillian fought to erase it.

"What was that town—the one that's so famous? I told my friend you lived there. She said she heard of it. It's where all the rich people live."

"Vista del Bravo," Gillian replied sadly. Once that name had made her heart sing. Now these mental journeys into the past brought a mix of pain and pleasure.

Stella had been searching around on top of her desk. It was cluttered with papers and ashtrays and coffee cups and other odds and ends of household debris. "I wrote out the receipt last night, right after you paid me. I'm forcing myself to be more efficient." She looked befuddled. Then she brightened. She reached for a small pad, her perplexed expression changing to one of satisfaction. "Here it is." She tore off a page and came back to Gillian, handing the receipt to her.

"Thanks." Gillian stuffed it into her purse, then turned to gather up her things.

"Hey, come on, I'll help you," Stella said, and lifted one of the boxes while Gillian took the suitcase. "Not that I want to see you go...."

Together the two women walked outside. Stella waited while Gillian opened the trunk of the light blue Ford Mustang. It was eighteen years old, but it still ran. All in all, it had been more faithful to her than Scott.

"I don't know why you gave up a nice house," Stella said, shaking her head again, as she put the box into the trunk and shoved it back to make room for what was to be added.

The thick adobe walls of the hotel had provided a barrier against the heat; outside, the sun was punishing. Gillian leaned into the trunk and settled the suitcase.

Stella continued. "If I had a man, let me tell you, some woman moves in on my territory, I don't ease on down the road...no way, Jose."

"Well, that's you. I'm me," Gillian said. Even to herself she sounded prissy and uptight and foolishly defensive. She tried to modulate her reaction. "It just never occurred to me to fight."

"Never *occurred* to you? Never *occurred* to you?" Stella's eyes were wide with mocking disbelief.

"No. I didn't think about, you know, making some kind of a big scene."

Stella exhaled noisily in a succinct expression of hopelessness.

"Well, look...the man didn't want me. He found someone else. It was pretty straightforward. Out with the old, in with the new. In California it happens all the time. With taco stands, roads, people. History is anything that lasts five minutes." Gillian ended with both her voice and arms raised.

But Stella persisted. "You never once thought to stand up for your rights?"

"No. I never thought. And I don't want to think about it now."

"Aye-yi-yi. You are such a case...." Stella rolled her eyes. "Why?" she asked bluntly, returning her gaze to Gillian.

For a second Gillian had no reply. She'd asked herself a lot of questions about her failed marriage, but never this one. "I didn't know I had any. I mean, I didn't have any experience with that sort of thing."

Stella Sanchez stared straight at her. She pointed her right index finger and said, "Look...you gotta learn to fight. Otherwise...in this world, see...you're finished."

The last word seemed to hang in the air.

"Well," said Gillian, turning and going inside to collect the other two boxes, "I don't have anything left to fight for."

"Next time, then," called Stella to her disappearing back.

Gillian returned, balancing the other two boxes one atop the other. She slipped them into the trunk, and Stella slammed it shut.

It was time to say goodbye. Gillian dreaded emotional scenes. Moving to the driver's side of the car, she opened the door and turned to Stella, who was hanging back slightly as if she too found last farewells unbearable.

"You know, if you ever wanted, you could write. I'd write back. We could keep in touch. Like maybe something big will happen and we'll want to tell each other. Hey...maybe I'll get married, right?" Stella was grinning from ear to ear. "Why not? It could happen."

"Right," said Gillian. "It could happen."

"Maybe you'll get married."

The taunt was meant to break the pain of parting.

"Yeah, well, only if I'm hit on the head and drugged and have no way of running in the opposite direction from the groom. Then, maybe...."

Stella laughed. "Around here we call that a bad attitude."

"I had a bad experience."

Suddenly the jokes turned sour. The past was still too much with Gillian and very real. Looking away from Stella in an attempt to hide her feelings, her eyes fell upon the shadow of San Geronimo. And what was San Geronimo but another reminder of the popular pastime of coupling for life?

Stella caught her glance. "Hey, did you hear that damn bell this afternoon?"

Gillian nodded. "John Proudfeather—he was ringing it for all he was worth."

"John Proudfeather? That was John Proudfeather up there?" Stella shook her head in consternation. "I should have known. What else? He's loco, that man. I'm singing, right? And all of a sudden these bells...screwing up my pitch. I can hardly hear myself sing. I've got it so I sound exactly like Linda Ronstadt. Did you know she's singing Spanish songs now? I think we look alike, what do you think?"

Stella briefly rearranged her face into a strange expression, then went on, "If we had a regular, full-time padre, then there'd be something to ring bells for. We wouldn't have to listen to some crazy bells in the middle of the day for nothing. We'd have regular events going on—christenings, weddings, formal deaths that you can dress up for. Not like now."

Gillian laughed. "People don't die here?"

"People don't do anything here. Except drink. And that they do way too much of."

They fell silent.

"Well, I've gotta take off," Gillian said, lowering her gaze.

"And they leave. People do that a lot, too." Stella sounded as though she was suspended between anger and misery.

Gillian wiped her dusty palm on the back of her jeans, careful to keep her eyes on the ground, away from Stella's face. She already knew Stella had tears in her eyes. And so did she.

"You write, huh?"

Gillian nodded, flicking her eyes briefly at the other woman; Stella had a wet streak on her cheek. Then, after a brief hug, she got into the eighteen-year-old Mustang, and Stella slammed the door shut with her knee. From her rearview mirror, Gillian could see Stella looking after her. She was still watching as she drove around the bend.

A cloud of thick sand trailed the Mustang as it bumped down the road in the direction of the main highway that would eventually take her through Santa Fe to Albuquerque. From there she would continue to California, and in California she would once again withdraw into the university's archives to search for a new subject on which to base her doctoral dissertation in cultural anthropology. With nothing else left in her life, she would become the high priestess of academia.

About a mile or so out of town, she caught sight of the stand of trees surrounding the trailer in which John Proudfeather lived, and next door to it, the more traditional abode dwelling that was home to the other two Indians whose lives Gillian had come to research for her thesis.

Outside the house of Maria Trujillo and Pablita Morningstar, a colorful line of wash had been hung out to dry. Maria was seventy-seven and Pablita eighty, yet age did not deter them from running their household with vigor. Silent and reclusive and dignified, they tended to their own lives. John, on the other hand, had a tendency to pop up everywhere, sometimes content to listen in the background, and at other times sharing his cryptic opinions, which were not always welcome.

When Gillian had asked the trio about their tribal history, they had all laughed. They had no history, John had insisted. Gillian had argued that everyone had a history, and John, as the only survivor of the Pachoas tribe, had a responsibility to his forefathers to record their mighty deeds for posterity.

This made John double up in hilarity. There were no mighty deeds, he informed her. If there had been acts of courage, he would not be the last Pachoan.

Likewise, Maria and Pablita were the only survivors of the Tuesan tribe. Their tribal history? They said that they had never paid attention. Maybe something had happened; maybe nothing. As for them, they couldn't remember anything that anyone would want to write about. Gillian, they said in their kindly manner, had very grand ideas of what their lives were about, but her illusions were just that—what she imagined wasn't real. They cooked and they cleaned. And as far as Indian magic went, they thought it was magic when they sold enough of their hand-loomed rugs to stock up with a month's supply of canned goods. Gillian, they suggested, should go in search of a showier tribe to research.

For one wild second, as Gillian passed by the Indian dwellings, she thought of making one last-ditch effort to fulfill the mission that had led her to Weed Junction. She could hear Stella Sanchez's voice telling her not to give up so easily. Stella was right, Gillian decided. Once more she would insist to the three ancient Indians that even they had to have within their cultures some fragment of wisdom and information to share with the world, something that could make the lives of others better or more complete.

But her foot remained on the gas pedal, and before she could make up her mind, the Mustang had passed the turnoff, the matter decided for her.

She had gone another mile when in the near distance she saw the beginnings of a dust devil. It grew off to the side of the road. It was small and harmless, yet, to Gillian, terribly fascinating in the way it seemed to rise out of nothing at all.

It was simply intoxicating to be in the presence of something that could not be predicted. Almost everything in life followed preordained patterns, but these oddities required more serious speculation.

Gillian slowed and bumped along, happily forgetting her problems and absorbed by the swirling phenomenon that danced over a few square feet of desert terrain.

By the time it took her to reach it, the little dust devil had grown larger, and had even set off on an adventure farther inland. Then it suddenly and unexpectedly came zipping back at a rapid clip, and in a leap crossed straight into Gillian's path.

Reflexively she slammed on her brakes.

It was an abrupt move, which in turn caused the car's engine to come to a sudden, lurching halt. In the next brief instant Gillian's immediate world was colored a golden tan by the traveling dust.

It all happened very quickly, coating her and the car with grit, and in the next moment the whirlpool of sand had skipped to the opposite side of the road and was happily spinning toward the Rio Grande.

Gillian watched it for a second, then leaned forward to reset the Mustang's ignition. New thoughts were already crowding into her mind as she turned her attention to the road before her.

And there she saw him—a man. A lone man in the blazing heat, with the sun behind him so that he was mostly just a dark shape silhouetted against the landscape.

He had on a hat. That much was clear. And it was possible to judge that beneath the hat he was tall and of a firm, strong build. Something tugged at her memory, something familiar about the man, something in the way he moved—the assured male gait, his arms swinging loose and easy by his sides, the slight hitch of his right shoulder every now and then.

She thought of the local cowboys who hung out at the Kachina Kantina, wondering if he was one of them, but her mind drew a blank.

Absorbed in the mental puzzle, Gillian leaned toward the windshield. Peering through the grime, she narrowed her eyes.

It can't be, she thought. In fact, the very idea was worth a laugh.

Impossible.

But the man was closer now, and this time she didn't laugh, because what couldn't possibly be . . . *was.*

Stella was going to faint.

Chapter Two

Deliverance was upon him.

The thought buoyed Kyle Dayton as he stood in the middle of the road, his feet on fire in the Tony Lama boots. Still, he hadn't been so happy to see anything since the time he had read his name on his first paycheck. Before him, maybe a hundred feet or so down the road, was a *car*.

The moment felt downright biblical in scope. He could see it played out on the silver screen: there he is, a weary soul lost in the desert, parched in body and downcast in spirit, when he sees far in the distance...a car.

Kyle abandoned the scenario, studying the situation in less dramatically colorful terms.

The vehicle before him was not moving, not even idling. But that, he quickly reassured himself, was only a technicality. Then something else caught his eye.

In his delight over the conveyance, Kyle hadn't noticed the woman staring at him. Now he did. Behind the dust-covered windshield there appeared to be a female form. She was sitting very still, watching him.

He raised his arm and effected a vigorous wave.

Through the clouded glass he saw the woman return the gesture—very tentatively.

Oh? A blah response? He would have thought a little enthusiasm was in order. How about a bit of excitement at seeing a movie star coming out of the desert void? He was in need of some goodwill.

He walked on. When he got to the car, he leaned down to the open window to address the driver, ready to get straight to the point. He had his plan. First off, he'd introduce himself; second, he would accept the invitation she'd offer to drop him at the nearest town. Once there, he'd treat himself to several ice-cold beers and arrange to have the truck serviced, after which he would continue with his immediate plans to locate a site for filming *Due West*.

With his agenda firmly in mind, he started with the first part of his greeting. "Hi, I'm—"

"Kyle Dayton," the woman said, putting no particular emphasis on his name.

He was still stooping slightly, bent at the waist, with both hands resting on his thighs as he peered in at her. "Thing of it is, I had a little trouble down the road," he went on, picking up the thread of his original script. The heat was making him light-headed. Or maybe it wasn't only the heat. "I think it's a busted radiator."

The woman was looking up at him with intense eyes.

Kyle stared back. *She was beautiful.*

He hadn't expected her to be beautiful. He hadn't expected anything at all. But if he had, it would have been to find behind the wheel some tough old desert rat with wiry-permed hair and leathery skin. No, he hadn't expected a woman like this at all. She had thick, wavy brown hair, darker than the brownish-green eyes by several degrees. A cheerfully beaded Indian headband in orange, yellow, green, blue and black was wrapped around her forehead.

"You can't be real," she stated, the hazel eyes still fixed on him, and by her expression still unimpressed by being favored with his movie-star persona in the middle of nowhere.

"Trust me," Kyle said. "I'm the genuine thing. Ask my feet. My feet wish they *weren't* real."

She smiled at that.

He smiled back, pleased.

The quiet surrounded them like an eavesdropper avid for the next interchange, which was not forthcoming.

He continued to find himself unbalanced by her attractiveness. Both their smiles had faded, and he tried to think of something to add to his last comment, but the thoughts he had were jumbled. He shifted position, standing up. It gave him something to do while he tried to pull himself together.

He reminded himself that he was a famous movie star and that millions of women were said to lust after him, but that didn't give him much of a boost, either.

His gaze swept the surroundings, but he saw nothing, his vision directed inward.

He tipped his Stetson down a little, stealing another look at the Mustang's driver. But she caught his glance, and so he followed through by leaning down again.

The hazel eyes presently looking into his were open and unprotected. He didn't read professional or monetary greed there. Nor did he pick up the usual sexual speculation. She was just surprised to see America's number one box office draw next to her car in the middle of the desert.

"This is crazy. I just can't believe this," she said, shaking her head from side to side. Her expression, both vocal and facial, was bemused. "I mean, you aren't supposed to be here. You're supposed to be..," She thought. "Somewhere else."

"Now that happens to be very true—very, very true indeed," Kyle said, glad that they were talking again. "You're absolutely right. I'm *not* supposed to be here. I'm supposed to be in an air-conditioned bar having a cold beer. But the important thing now is that *you*'re real and *you*'re here. But I don't suppose your car has air conditioning, does it?" he hinted broadly. A crooked smile took possession of one side of his potential benefactor's face. Even while being cooked by the New Mexico sun, he thought she looked fetching.

She shook her head, and her tone was self-effacing as she confessed, "Sorry. It doesn't work. The radio doesn't even work. The car's old, not too reliable. It's an investment. Someday," she said, exaggerating her statement so that anger and humor mingled in the message, "I'm going to make a real killing on this classic piece of..." She slapped the steering wheel with the flat of her hand. More evenly she continued, "Most of the time the air conditioning doesn't matter. I roll down the windows and drive a hundred miles an hour."

"Yeah," said Kyle. "Hundred-mile clip ought to work up a nice breeze for you." He was a little irritated about the air not working and realized it had probably come across in his voice. He didn't enjoy being mean, especially when he was kicking someone who was obviously already down. And besides, it didn't pay to alienate his only hope for a ride to his beer.

More magnanimously he said, "Well, so what? Fresh air's great. And there's enough noise in the world, anyway. Who needs a radio?" He glanced down the length of the vehicle. "You've got wheels. And that's what counts."

The hazel eyes dropped lower, thick dark lashes shadowing the tanned skin. "There seems to be a slight problem in this area, too."

Kyle watched her lean forward and try the ignition. The car didn't start.

He couldn't believe it. Maybe she was right: he wasn't real and this wasn't happening. The sun seemed almost unbearable now that his situation had taken this further turn for the worse.

She sank back against the seat and restlessly tapped her fingers against the steering wheel.

"Yeah," Kyle agreed. "See what you mean. That's a problem, all right." With a heartfelt grimace, he stepped back from the car and, straightening to his full height of six foot two, looked into their vast, desolate surroundings as he began to wonder what he should do.

"Sorry," she offered. "For whatever that's worth. You're probably very disappointed. Things like this probably don't happen to famous movie stars."

"Not every day." Kyle stared at the mountains rising on the horizon. The huge monuments of nature made him feel small and transitory. Mountains put life into clearer perspective.

"Hey, it's nothing," he said, speaking into the desert emptiness. "Lighten up. A busted engine can happen to anyone. In fact, it just did—to both of us." He considered sharing his insight about the mountains with her, wondering if she would understand. But that seemed too pushy, not to mention too intimate. Instead he said, "It's not your fault. Anyway, we'll just wait here a few minutes and probably a car'll pass and we'll hitch a ride and it'll all end happily."

She didn't say anything, obviously not believing in his fantasy, but not cruel enough to destroy it. He didn't believe it either, but his feet hurt too much to set off again so soon.

Kyle looked back at her, and once more found himself absorbed by her appearance. She possessed a startling, open beauty. It was not a raw appeal in the crude sense that she exuded; it was more a vulnerability, a softness one did not often find in people these days.

"So here we are," he said with ironic good cheer, and gestured broadly, taking in the hundred miles or so around them. "The two of us. The sun. And busted cars. Not a pretty situation perhaps, but certainly challenging. My truck broke down back there," Kyle explained. He looked down the road, gauging the length of his trek, and went on as if she had asked a question. "I don't know, a couple of miles back or so. In the heat, on foot, it seems more like it had to have been a hundred." He looked back down to the Mustang's driver. "I'll—we'll—have to get to a service station. Think I'm asking for another miracle?"

She nodded, her eyes thoughtful. "The next thing to one. Weed Junction's the nearest town. There's no service station, but a guy there—Billy Riggs—fixes cars sometimes."

"Weed Junction, huh?" Kyle laughed. "Really? You don't mean *the* Weed Junction?"

"The place isn't any better than the name."

"I'm sure it was an oversight, but it wasn't on the map."

"Waste of good ink, I guess. People tend not to stop in Weed Junction."

"Except some who are extra lucky and break down in the desert. Must be quite a place."

"It was an accident to begin with. A couple of sharpies from Philadelphia came by in the mid-eighteen hundreds and gobbled up a lot of the land for themselves, saying the railroad was going to pass by and there'd be a stop there. When word got around, everyone wanted in on the fortune that was bound to be made. Then, when everyone was sufficiently feverish, the two crooks concocted this story that one of them was gravely ill and they had to sell out. Anyway, buildings were built and people waited for the railroad...."

"Which of course never came."

"Oh, it came—a hundred and fifty miles off, where it had originally been scheduled to run. And just for the record, Weed Junction wasn't its original name. In the beginning it was called Glory. Can you believe it? Glory?" She shook her head, looking slightly sadder. "But after the railroad thing went bust, people started to refer to it as a place where only weeds would grow. Poor old Weed Junction. There's not much left of it now but a handful of buildings, and some drifters and people who probably wouldn't fit in most other places. Every once in a while a tourist gets lured into town by the sign. They have a beer and stop at the rock shop if it's open, and if any of the Indians are around, they'll sell them some rugs or jewelry. Only the jewelry John Proudfeather sells is made in Taiwan. Another Weed Junction secret."

Kyle raised his brows. "Sign?"

"Everyone misses it. It's on the highway, but not placed prominently enough for anyone to see."

"I saw a peeling billboard advertising a coffee shop in Taos, and I saw a dirt road that looked like it didn't go anywhere near civilization—which is why I took it."

The slanted smile returned again and the hazel eyes softened and became alight with private thoughts as if she were visualizing more than she described. "Behind the coffee shop sign there's the famous historical Weed Junction marker. The Weed Junction Indian War, circa 1888."

"Very impressive. If not a railroad, at least a real Indian war."

"Unfortunately, no. At the very most it was a skirmish, a spat. There were two tribes—the Pachoans and the Tuesans." She stopped and directed the green-brown eyes his way without fully turning her face towards him. "Heard of them?"

Kyle considered the names. "No," he stated emphatically.

"No one has—or hardly anyone. If you really look, like I did, you can find minor references alluding to their presence. Anyway, the sign says they got into a battle over horses, but that wasn't right either. They were mules. Nobody won the alleged battle, and the mules ended up running off into the hills. In fact, the tribes were hardly legitimate tribes in the traditional sense. They were actually offshoot bands of Apache and Navaho Indians from way, way back."

"But the marker stays there anyway?"

"It was put there by an historical society. They mean well."

"Only it never happened. So isn't that a little misleading to the public?"

"Oh, the ladies in the historical society don't know that it's all just a myth. Hardly anyone does. And the people around here who do know, don't care. They're comfortable with legends. They build them up and tear them down every day, depending on their mood or how much they've drunk."

"I'll be taking quite a secret to the grave."

"Are you kidding? I saw *Cast Iron*. You crossed the Alps on skis while being chased by a mad killer in a helicopter, and were still able to make love to that blonde with the green, slanted eyes in Monte Carlo a few hours later. A walk down a dirt road couldn't possibly finish you off."

Kyle smiled. "I don't see any snow. Or a blonde," he added innocently, just to test the waters a bit.

"Pretend," she said, then added quickly, "about the snow."

"Look, I don't want to disillusion you or anything, but in real life movie stars get blisters."

"Then you'll love the moleskin in my trunk."

It was the first time Kyle had been able to get a full view of his rescuer. She left her post by the steering wheel and moved around to the back of the Mustang. He followed and stood to one side, watching as she opened the trunk and began to sift through a box of what appeared to be personal items—some clothes, miscellaneous toiletries, a couple of paperback books. She was either leaving home or going home; either way, she was traveling light. The shorts she wore revealed long, tanned legs. Her waist was small and her hips rounded. Under ordinary circumstances notions of sex might have swept his mind clear of other thoughts, but under present conditions the vision of a cold beer was the most he could physically handle.

"Here we go," she said triumphantly, and pulled out a small white and red plastic first aid kit, which she raised high in the air as if exhibiting a trophy. The sun shone in her hair, making her look softly angelic. "Take off your boots and we'll get you fixed up."

Take off your clothes and I'll make you a star. The words ran through his mind, their cadence the same as those she had spoken.

As a man, he sensed instantly how easy it would be to use such an innocent; he'd seen the Hollywood sharks of the entertainment business do it a thousand times to pliable young women new to the scene. And as a man, he also knew the woman in his presence could inspire the opposite emotion, that of protectiveness. It would all depend upon the man, on his character. At the moment she was safe; he was far too tired to have any character, good or bad.

His feet had swollen, and it was hard to pull off the Tony Lamas. She saw him struggling and put down the first aid kit to help him.

"Okay, tense up," she ordered, and grabbed one heel as he leaned against the side of the Mustang for support. The boot slipped off.

She stumbled back a couple of feet, and they both laughed. She was even prettier when she smiled. But the good humor died away soon enough, and sadness was left in its place. He wondered about her troubles, then told himself to forget it; they were ships passing in the night.

"Here," she said, and cut off a patch of moleskin, which she handed to him for his sore heel.

He wobbled as he stood on one leg, and she came to his side, offering her support. Her arm was hardly enough to hold him, but he took the help anyway. He liked touching her. There was a kind of intimacy involved in everything they did. Probably it was due to the remoteness of their surroundings.

And then, for the first time, he consciously wondered who she was—not just her name, but *who* she was. Where did she come from and why? Where was she going and why? "You know, if I live to have another beer, I'm planning on putting you in my will. So who should I make out the millions to?"

"Oh," she said, looking up from her work. "Sorry...I completely forgot. Gillian. Gillian Mc-

Guire." She smiled briefly, perfunctorily, and went on with what she was doing.

"...pleasure," said Kyle, thinking she had a beautiful smile and a beautiful body, and that if this had been one of his movies, they'd be spending the night together in the next scene. And that would definitely coincide with pleasure.

Maybe that was all he said, the one word, but in the way he said it something more of what he felt must have been conveyed, because she looked up again, suddenly surprised, as if responding to his thoughts. Their eyes held, and she looked down again, barely murmuring, "...pleased," in return.

This is a dangerous man, Gillian cautioned herself. She cautioned herself not to even think about him. She should just do what she had to do—put on the moleskin, get them both to Weed Junction, get the Mustang patched up and get on with her life.

Once the repair work was completed and the Tony Lamas back in place, Kyle Dayton stomped around in a small circle, testing the result of their efforts.

"So?" Gillian asked, watching. "Think you can make it down the road?"

Kyle shook his head. "No."

Gillian laughed. "Come on. Lawrence crossed the Sahara."

"That was a movie."

"Based on real life."

Kyle grimaced. "You're a hard woman."

Gillian looked at him, wishing it were true. Her life would be a whole lot better. "You noticed," she said, enjoying the private irony.

Chapter Three

The longest, hottest hour Gillian had ever known, that was what it took to cover the distance from the ailing Mustang into town.

Along the route, the landscape had assumed surrealistic qualities. Everything was dwarfed by the endless ocean of blue sky that stung the eyes with its purity—even the mountains. Far off—was it really that far?—tall white clouds began to build and tumble over the ridges of pale red mountains, and closer—were they really so close?—small colonies of cottonwoods stood like old, twisted men conversing among themselves, watching the passage of the two travelers.

For the first twenty minutes of their safari, she and Kyle had made pleasant and determined small talk. For whatever their respective reasons, Gillian felt they were both deliberately intent on keeping their comments off the personal. They spoke about the terrain. They conversed about the kind of food one was likely to encounter in the Southwest region, the consensus being that what passed for good meant in actuality "a lot on one plate." They critiqued the Santa Fe Opera.

And all these interchanges seemed artificial, stilted, and perhaps even cowardly.

But soon enough, even these superficial social pleasantries were abandoned. It took all their effort just to breathe and set one foot before the next.

In the end, both kept their own counsel, finishing off the last miserable stretch of their walk still locked in silence, and entered the so-called city limits of Weed Junction precisely one hour after they had abandoned the Mustang.

Out of the blinding light and into the lobby of the Weed Junction Hotel they stumbled, only to find themselves blinded now by the comparatively cool darkness furnished by the thick adobe walls.

For a moment, like pilgrims reaching the shore, they stood just inside the door, taking stock of their good fortune. A wooden fan rotated above them, creaking.

"Holy...moly...!"

Gillian followed the sound until her eyes focused on Carrie Riggs, sitting with her wiry body scrunched into the corner of the cracked, maroon leather sofa. Carrie had a standing job to watch the hotel every afternoon, when Stella took her break and went across the street for some gossip and her afternoon libation at the Kachina Kantina. At the moment, Carrie's blue-jeaned knees were up, supporting a month-old issue of *Soap Opera Digest*.

"Hey, Carrie...." Gillian greeted her wearily.

The magazine flopped to the floor as Carrie pulled herself up. "Gillian...hi...I thought you had headed outa here...." Her words trailed disconnectedly one after the other, the tone echoing with the amazement associated with sightings of visitors from outer space.

"I thought so, too. But things kind of happened to change that."

"Yeah, man...." Carrie looked wild-eyed, a person ready to jump out of her skin. Now her attention was fully clamped on Kyle.

"Hi," Kyle said, his voice mellow and distinctive, sounding just as it did in those thousand-seat movie theaters. He touched his hat brim, the gesture easy, unself-conscious, a man obviously accustomed to women coming unglued in his presence. To Gillian, the lack of pomp only added to his personal magnetism.

She hated liking him; even being smitten would have been preferable to liking him. Being smitten implied an emotional distance caused by an unreal vision. But if you *liked* a man, you were dealing on an entirely different level altogether, one that smacked of the possibility of establishing something concrete.

"Hi," Carrie breathed, and bravely added, "Kyle..." with the air of someone who was already recording the unbelievable situation in order to repeat it, along with embellishments, to others later on.

"Is Billy around?" Gillian asked. "Both our cars are on the blink. If he could take a look at them, we—"

Carrie shook her head. "Forget *that*." Her ponytail whipped back and forth behind her. "Ol' Billy Dean

Riggs just took himself off about three hours ago. And I don't care to see him again if I live to be three hundred and fifty years old,'' she finished with a lilting, passionate bitterness. At least for a moment she seemed to forget Kyle's presence as she flounced over to the hotel's registration desk and brought out the cigar box that contained the room keys. "So... looks to me like you're going to have to stay the night then. Seeing as how no one from Santa Fe's going to come out till tomorrow, anyways."

"Oh," said Gillian, seeing ahead. "Well... that's really too bad." She was thinking more in terms of herself and Kyle, rather than commenting on Carrie's marital dispute, but Carrie didn't know that.

"No, it's not. It's great. I don't need him. I got an uncle who says he can teach me how t'drive a big rig like his, and I can make major bucks doing long hauls. Ol' Billy Dean can just sit around with his stupid rock shop for all I care, cracking geodes in two and strumming his guitar."

Carrie was twenty-three, with a complexion that remained paler than oatmeal no matter what the sun was doing. With her drab hair and her limpid blue eyes, her appearance was a study in monotony. Yet, as if in compensation for her lack of external vibrancy, her temperament was mercurial and intense. Gillian and everyone else knew that she was crazy about Billy, and the only trouble was that Billy was periodically driven crazy *by* Carrie, thus necessitating his periodic flights from Weed Junction. Unfortunately, for Gillian's present purpose, this particular flight was inconvenient.

Gillian turned to Kyle. "See, they have these fights. Billy takes off. He's gone for a few days and then comes back."

"Encouraging," commented Kyle. His expression read aggravation. "A few days, huh?"

"No sweat," Carrie said. "I'll call a station in Santa Fe. They'll send a truck out tomorrow. You'll get towed back into the city, and everything'll work out. You can be on your way...." The last was said with markedly less enthusiasm.

"Sounds good to me," Kyle said. "I'd be extremely grateful if you could arrange that."

"What's he *doing* here?" Carrie whispered furtively to Gillian, as if Kyle wouldn't notice their interchange.

"He's..." The truth was, Gillian didn't know. She looked to Kyle, suddenly curious herself. What *was* America's favorite movie star doing in the middle of the New Mexico desert?

"A beer. I came for a beer," Kyle said.

Carrie arched one pale eyebrow and drew in her chin. "A beer?"

"A cold beer."

"Oh, for sure...." It was Carrie's idea of a challenge.

"Really. I'm very sure," he said. "So you'll excuse me?" He edged his way closer to the door, as if drawn by a magnet to the Kachina across the way. "Care to join me?" His gray eyes had fallen on Gillian.

Gillian hesitated. A scenario captured her thoughts. She was drunk on beer, laughing and hanging onto Kyle as they danced close together. She saw his eyes, gray and intense. And then, shifting suddenly as in a dream, they were on a bed, Kyle shirtless, lowering himself over her and— "No," Gillian said, her heart thumping against her breast. It would be so easy to... "Thanks, but no." She had to force the words out.

She burned with embarrassment, certain that Kyle was looking at her a beat longer than was necessary. He must have read her thoughts and was deciding if he cared enough to press for an advantage.

Then he nodded and said, "Ladies...adios." He made a satirical and attractive show of tipping his Stetson, then exited from their presence.

With Kyle gone, the room suddenly seemed safer to Gillian, but also less bright.

Carrie let out a howl and feigned a dramatic swoon, then began hopping around with both arms flapping at her sides. "I can't believe it. I can't believe it! I...can't...believe...it!"

"Same room?" Gillian asked, identifying all too well with Carrie's sentiments.

"What? Yeah, your room, Gillian—sheets are already changed," Carrie said, stopping her wild leaps and tossing the key over to her. "My God, Gillian.... Kyle Dayton. What's he *doing* here? In Weed Junction? My God!"

"He's broken down—just like the rest of us, I guess," Gillian commented wryly, and started up the stairs.

"Gillian..."

Gillian stopped, then looked over her shoulder to Carrie who wore a distant, drifty expression.

"I'm seriously in love with that man."

Gillian nodded. "You and half the female population of the world."

"That's okay," Carrie said. "I can deal with competition. Love like this is powerful—it knows no bounds."

"Which soap opera's that from?"

Carrie grinned. "My own. I made it up. It sounds good, huh?"

"You're wasting your talents here."

"Gillian..."

"Yes, Carrie?"

"He's...like, incredible. Really. He's got flecks. Gold flecks in gray eyes, just like in the movies. And look at you. You're so calm. Doesn't he *do* anything to you?"

"He hasn't tried yet. But maybe he was too tired. Most movie stars find me irresistible."

Carrie giggled, and for that Gillian was immeasurably relieved. Kyle Dayton's presence in her life had brought a lot of unwanted emotions to the surface.

Gillian started up the stairs again, but this time stopped and turned on her own, asking, "Doesn't John Proudfeather work on engines sometimes with Billy?"

"Yeah, sometimes he does. Only you gotta find him first. That's the trouble with men round here. Unreliable and unpredictable. And gone."

"And good riddance to them all," Gillian said, the light amusement in her voice at odds with the ache that flowed over her as she thought again of Scott and the mythical marriage in which she had believed.

"When Kyle leaves Weed Junction, I'm going to die," Carrie called morosely to the ascending Gillian. "This is the biggest thing that ever happened to me! I'll never get over him—never!"

Carrie was just carrying on, but even so Gillian knew too much about endings to be able to joke back. She continued silently up the stairs, as if she hadn't heard or been touched by the words, and was glad to close the door of room #2 against a world that constantly reminded her of things she wanted to forget.

Kyle downed his second Dos XX, then ordered one more. Already he was feeling good.

The Kachina Kantina was everything he had dreamed of and more. Whereas life generally turned out to be less than one fantasized, Weed Junction was becoming the ultimate realization of all his boyhood hopes and dreams. The place might have been a set out of one of his favorite old Western movies . . . *complete with a beautiful woman*.

Into a mind relaxed by alcohol an image of Gillian McGuire insinuated itself, taking on realistic contours. Leisurely he abandoned himself to the mindless, hedonistic pleasures of an erotic daydream. He saw the face with the compelling greenish-brown eyes and the clothed body that he would like to view unwrapped. Then magically, rounded curves and contoured valleys of flesh, shorn of inhibiting garments, appeared before him.

He was a master of the daydream. It was a talent honed to perfection during childhood days and nights spent alone, longing for something better. Now he could make anything happen in one of his mental productions, and inserting himself into the next frame, he did just that. He first took Gillian McGuire standing up against a wall, then on a bed with her slim, tanned legs wrapped tightly around him, and again with her thick, golden-brown hair trailing over the edge of the bed. She was incredible, responsive, yielding. And he was . . . well, simply fantastic.

The daydream swirled, changing moods.

He was over her, in her, his hands on either side of her lovely face as he said he loved her. The green-brown eyes drank in his words, reflecting her own feelings of love for him. Now it was no longer sex. Now as he moved against her, it was something more, something so exquisite that—   The gossamer world splintered.

Something cold washed over Kyle, a sensation of regret that twisted itself into fear, which in turn evolved less frighteningly into a feeling of abject foolishness.

Fool that he was! It wasn't the first time he had been swept away by such lapses into acute romanticism. But he knew how to bound back into the real world, and immediately, skillfully and protectively avoided deeper discomfort by plunging himself into an intellectual analysis of his escapist tendencies.

Okay. What was real and what wasn't? Was this something personal—this "thing" he had for the McGuire woman?

He sipped thoughtfully on his third Dos XX.

Or was he merely reacting to a subliminal stimulus, memories intruding from his boyhood?

On the other hand, maybe what he had here was totally biological—a man with hot feet might also have hot pants. That notion certainly fitted.

He suddenly realized he had reached bottom on the beer, and signaled the bartender for a fourth. He needed fuel for thought.

The beer came, and he grabbed the bottle and drank a quarter of the cold liquid, as if it held the courage he lacked.

Once he had loved a woman—it had been a pure, wholehearted love. He had trusted. He had believed. And he had been fooled. It had happened a long, long time ago, but even if he waited another million years, time would not diminish the bitter memory of the days and weeks and months that had grown into years when he had waited by a window, a small boy then, his eyes boring through the glass, gray eyes with flecks of gold like question marks, eyes that searched for a woman who never came back to claim him.

The memory stabbed at him, and practiced in dulling himself against the old, endless hurt, Kyle forced his mind to be still. He finished his fourth beer. The bartender sent him a questioning look; Kyle nodded. Why not tie one on? Besides, it was hot and he was thirsty.

He swiveled to the side, keeping one foot on the bar's brass railing while he took in the action around him. No one paid him any notice.

Gathered in groups throughout the cantina, they were a lively bunch, and he was happy with his present anonymity, more than content to be a fly on the wall, listening in to real people living real lives. He had spent more hours than he cared to count being bored by deal makers in the Polo Lounge, their wrists weighed down by Rolex watches, their minds laden with figures preceded by dollar signs.

Reality had hit him on the day that a doctor had filled him in on his chances in life, using a six-letter word—the *C* word. At the time he hadn't viewed his situation as lucky; but in retrospect and having been the victor, he could see he had been fortunate. While others negotiated deals that had no meaning beyond a new Jaguar, he would live for what had lasting value, not wasting what remained of his life. And who knew how long that would be? The doctor had given him a clean bill of health, but there were no guarantees that what he had been granted was anything more than a temporary reprieve. But even if he had no more than one year, that would be enough; he would be able to write his own epitaph. It would be *Due West*.

A peal of throaty female laughter dislodged the heavy thoughts. Kyle caught sight of a vibrant woman, probably in her late twenties, holding court across the room among a group of men seated at a round table. Her hair was coal black, her dark eyes flashing beacons as she gesticulated broadly, regaling her audience with a tale.

Someone called her name: Stella.

Another man reached out, and grabbing her by the waist, pulled her onto his lap.

She was dressed flamboyantly, the outfit she wore incongruous with the surroundings. Kyle saw the full breasts jounce above the Hawaiian print sarong as she struggled against her captor for an instant, before settling into the man's embrace. He kissed the side of her neck, one hand rising over the rib cage, a finger exploring just below the full curve of bosom, and the woman—Stella—smiled, her body melding further into the man's larger frame. The brittle gaiety of her expression had likewise softened into sexual longing.

Suddenly the moment was laced with an overpowering eroticism as the air in the saloon swirled with smoke and music, talk and laughter. Over the jukebox a male voice sang about feelings—a woman named Ruby was going out the door, heading for trouble, heading for love. The bass guitar strummed in time to the universal beat of mounting sexual passion.

It was impossible not to be affected. A tide of sweet and painful and urgent desire washed through Kyle. He swallowed hard, fighting against the raw male energy as he turned away and clamped his hand hard on the neck of the new bottle of beer placed before him.

It had been a long time since he had been with a woman.

It had been an even longer time since he had wanted—truly wanted—any woman with whom he had lain.

The truth was that he wanted to be absorbed by a woman, to offer himself to her, to take her, hold her, know her, every particle of himself joining with her.

But there wasn't such a woman in his life, and to take a substitute for what he yearned—even to have the tempting Gillian McGuire, who had been the subject of his heated and acrobatic thoughts during his early beers—was not going to be satisfactory. The laughter and music continued behind him.

It was after his fourth beer that he was discovered. The woman in the Hawaiian print dress gave a yelp.

Kyle knew that sound from long experience, and turned his head to see Stella extricate herself from her admirer's embrace. Kyle watched with resignation and amused fascination as she came swinging toward him on high, thin, backless heels.

"Well, hot damn," she exclaimed robustly. "Welcome to Weed Junction, U.S. of A." And with that, she extended her hand. "Stella Sanchez," she introduced herself, then rushed on, "Mr. Kyle Dayton...what on earth brings you to parts as forlorn and godforsaken as this?"

He smiled, liking her. She had no airs. She wasn't coy. She wasn't shy. "Destiny, I guess." He had meant to be politely evasive, but the answer seemed surprisingly apt. He shook the hand with its red-lacquered nails, two of which he couldn't help but notice bore miniature decals, one a fat cherub, reminiscent of Cupid, the other being a teddy bear.

And then he was surrounded.

A man with longish hair and a bandanna draped loosely around his weathered neck ordered a round of beers for everyone. There was a communal toast to Kyle. And that was it, more or less; after that, he might just as well have been a sheepherder come in from the hills for all the notice he got. He was just one among a lot of other men with their boots resting on the bar's brass foot railing, torsos pressed against the counter's lip, half listening to Johnny Cash wail about walking a straight line for love, while they cracked crude jokes among themselves about old, fat girlfriends and the time someone ate too many beans.

Kyle told a story or two himself.

Sometime later he was into his seventh beer and feeling no pain. He was vaguely aware that his feet were still sore, but it didn't matter much. The rest of him was happy. The heat was worse now in the late part of the day; but that, too, seemed inconsequential in view of the satisfaction he felt. Overhead an old wooden fan made a different kind of music as it struggled to stir up the heavy air, though it actually did little more than annoy flies that ventured too near the creaking blades.

He was pleasantly high.

In fact it seemed after all the beers that anything was possible in life, and as his gaze traveled the room, taking in the activity, he realized how deeply grateful he was to be alive, to be as Stella Sanchez had phrased it, "in this godforsaken place."

Across the room, the desert twilight was stealing through the salts of the double, swinging doors. The softness startled him, rearranging his senses so that all at once the noise and smoke of the saloon were no longer pleasant. A moment later, as Willie Nelson was singing about all the women he had loved and left, Kyle pushed through the saloon's doors into the pastel world beyond.

For a moment he paused on the wooden porch, affected by the fading beauty of the world. The mountains beyond the town were purple and magenta, dark shadows already sliding into huge crevices.

His eyes moved downward, summoned by the sign of the Weed Junction Hotel, which, dangling from two rusty hinges, whined in a breeze.

Then another movement caught his attention. A form in a second-story window shifted as his eyes made contact.

Gillian McGuire.

He stared at the window, thinking, and then, seven beers crazy, he set off across the dirt track that was Weed Junction's only thoroughfare.

In the lobby, the girl—Carrie Riggs—handed him his key. She stared at him, into him, just as so many other women had devoured him, heated speculations about his sexual prowess shining in their eyes.

"Thanks," he said, and she stuttered something in return. Behind him, he was certain the girl was melting into a sea of erotic fantasies as he made his way up the stairs to the second floor.

The Tony Lamas sounded harsh against the plank flooring of the second-story corridor. In contrast, delicate light spilled into the hallway from small windows at either end of the hall, filling the space in which he moved with an amber mist.

The beers and heat and strange surroundings had brought forth a curious combination of divergent emotions. Kyle felt both reckless and sentimental. And as he came nearer the door behind which Gillian McGuire could be found, feelings entirely foreign to his nature erupted inside him.

The brass #2 nailed against the door gleamed golden in the ocher light. Two. That magical number of union. His mind burned through the wooden barrier, behind which Gillian McGuire remained a separate, female *one*. He saw her again in his imagination, unclothed, her breasts high and small, alabaster where the sun had not touched. So real was the vision that he caught his breath, desire choking him. The legs were tanned and long, the hips flared, curving into smooth buttocks over which he would run his fingers. . . .

His gaze traveled absently down the hallway, and suddenly he was looking through the small window, where the light had now faded into a melancholy shade of indigo.

The color pulled him back in time. He was a small boy again, his face immobile as he looked beyond the front window of his aunt's white frame bungalow in Clearwater, the Florida light settling into that haunted shade of blue from which his mother had never emerged.

Feelings assaulted him, and saving himself, Kyle snapped his head away from the sight of the sky. The golden #2 before him was no longer magical; it represented only pain.

The Tony Lamas bore him swiftly to the next door, where he turned the key in the lock. Stepping into the empty room, sparsely furnished in heavily shellacked pine, he slipped wearily onto his bed, safely alone.

In the next room, carefully guarded by the #2, he could dimly make out the sounds of Gillian McGuire going about routine tasks. Then the tub was being filled in her bathroom. He could picture her in his mind, imagine how she would look unclothed and accessible. He closed his eyes, but the beautiful picture didn't go away, not even when sleep claimed him.

One minute after placing her head on the pillow of her reclaimed bed, Gillian fell into a deep slumber.

And for two hours she was spared the several troubles and conscious turmoil of her life. She did not think of Scott and their failed relationship. She did not dwell upon the thesis that she had to write, for which she currently had no subject. She could blissfully forget that her funds were dwindling daily.

She also did not think any more about her attraction to Kyle Dayton.

But then, two hours later she awoke, and the world came pressing back in on her.

The first thing to affect her was the heat. The room was stifling, and still in a sleep-logged state, she listlessly left the bed to stand by the window, just in case a breeze should happen by.

It was then that she saw him.

Across the street, the double doors of the Kachina Kantina suddenly swung open—and into a twilight that was rapidly turning from pink to a deep golden hue stepped Kyle Dayton, much as if he had emerged from a dream she had been having.

He did not move forward, but remained where he was on the crude plank flooring outside the saloon. Enfolded in twilight, he seemed to take in the countryside, and as he did so Gillian could not move her own eyes from him.

He was an extraordinary man. She hated herself for that admission as it made her feel foolish, in her own mind placing her in the same category as Carrie and God only knew how many others on the planet.

But it was true. If he was a movie star, beloved by women throughout the world, it was because there was something remarkable about him. The special quality he exuded was not just his physical attractiveness, although it would be impossible for her to deny that he was handsome. He was tall with broad shoulders. There was an unstructured carelessness about his person that translated into sheer masculinity. His hair was a dusty brown with blond highlights, and he wore it short enough to be combed neatly, but long enough to be mussed easily.

In the face she studied from the window, it seemed that soft edges met hard ones: the angle of jaw was clean and sharp, but gentled by the curve of the lower cheek. The high ridge of his cheekbones accented eyes that told conflicting stories. In short, he threatened to be not only a movie star, but a real man of complex nature.

Kyle shifted the focus of his attention and suddenly faced the hotel, just at the moment she was about to step aside, having forgotten that she too could be as easily observed in the window as the man in the street.

But it was too late.

His eyes caught hers, and as if struck by a beam of pure energy, she realized with a shock that they wanted each other—that even in the afternoon as they'd walked in silence, emotions had been building that had led to this moment of understanding.

But not of acceptance.

Backing away, Gillian stumbled blindly from the window, and despite the heat stood shivering in the yellow crop top and bikini pants.

She moved about the room, doing things that had no meaning, washing an unused ashtray, opening and closing drawers that once had held her few belongings, as if she might find some leftover scraps of herself.

A moment later, she heard footsteps in the hall. They paused just beyond her room. She stared at the wooden barrier, her heart beating so hard that she felt it must be heard on the other side of the door. If he were to knock, she would let him in.

Then the danger was over. He passed, his steps moving down the hall. She heard his door close and the muffled sounds of boots across the floor. And then nothing.

A moment later she sank into a tub of cool water, sealing herself off from the heat that had nothing to do with the temperature outside. Closing her eyes, she vowed that she was going to get out of Weed Junction without having to see Kyle Dayton again.

Chapter Four

So," Gillian finished, her mouth as dry from nerves as from the long walk, "do you think you could help me out?"

Up to this point her eyes had been focused on John Proudfeather's face as she spoke her piece. Now she could feel the assertive strength she had mustered to direct the course of her life begin to ebb. She looked down, emotionally spent.

John Proudfeather sat outside his trailer on a low pile of dried logs left over from the last winter. His red shirt was wrinkled, the sleeves rolled up to the elbows, the tails hanging over the faded jeans he wore. What once must have been a mane of coarse black hair was now a rough blend of salt and pepper strands. As usual, he wore it drawn into a tail at the nape and fas-

tened with a loop of deerskin. His own gaily colored
Taiwan beaded headband circled his forehead.

Gillian waited for him to respond to her plea for assistance. There was nothing to do but wait. From experience, she knew John wasn't the type who could be
rushed into doing or saying anything.

The patch of earth on which she stood was mottled
by pools of silvery light drifting through an over-
hanging bough. Some minutes before, a faint breeze
had sprung up, disorienting her as it continually
shifted. Each time, an image of Kyle Dayton as he had
appeared to her from the window of her room took
advantage of her momentary lapse of concentration.
As before, the gray eyes found hers, and again her
heart felt the sudden sharp sting—part pleasure, part
fear—as their minds touched and melded. Then,
blessedly, Kyle's image faded.

She wondered if John Proudfeather had bought her
story about having an appointment in Los Angeles as
her excuse for the urgency to leave town. It had
sounded good to her. Sometimes John could be contrary just to be contrary, and it didn't pay to give him
any kind of an edge. The truth was always an advantage.

Shards of moonlight fell onto the craggy planes of
his face as he peered into the distance. His trailer and
the adobe home shared by Pablita Morningstar and
Maria Trujillo were surrounded by a stand of old cottonwoods planted purposely to break the forces of
wind and light. But tonight there was only gentleness
as the leaves whispered softly in the warm air.

Gillian remained quiet, chewing on the inside of her lip as she waited for John to say something encouraging. Finally he gave a single nod.

Gillian's mood lightened. She was saved. With John to fix her car, she'd be getting out of Weed Junction early tomorrow morning and wouldn't have to deal with her attraction to Kyle Dayton.

"Good," she said quickly, as if to lock in their verbal contract, adding, "Thanks, John. I really appreciate it. Carrie said you've worked with Billy a lot and it won't be anything for you to figure out the problem."

John's dark eyes turned toward her. "I'll take a look at it tomorrow afternoon."

Gillian's good mood plunged several stories down a long elevator shaft. "But I really have to get out of here...."

John grunted. "Have something of my own to do early."

"Well, maybe it could wait?"

John shook his head.

"Is it something I could help you with? Maybe we could get it done together early, and then you'd have time to take a look at my Mustang?"

"I was going for a walk," John said in his soft and deep voice, the words measured, as if he had said something profound.

She stared at him, trying to decide if he was being deliberately mean or if he was just joking, playing with her to make her beg and squirm. Then again, it could easily be that John was crazy, as Stella always insisted.

"Well, John...couldn't the walk wait a while? I mean you can take a walk any day, whereas I have this appointment...."

He shook his head.

"Why?" she asked, trying hard to hold back her exasperation.

"Why can't the car wait?" he asked, looking at her queerly.

With absolute certainty, Gillian realized that John was not crazy. He was not stupid, either. He was insightful. He had known from the beginning that there was more to her lame story than she was letting on. John was a con artist, and like any con artist, he didn't like to be taken.

He broke his discomforting gaze then and stared into the dark again, as if he had forgotten her entirely. With his face streaked with silver light and the shadows smoothing out the lines of time, just for a moment Gillian imagined him as a young brave, painted for war—a man John had never been.

When she had asked him about his life, hoping for input for her thesis, he hadn't wanted to talk about it. But gradually she had pried out a few odd revelations. According to John, there had been no chance for drama in his life, no call for heroic deeds, no mountains to scale.

For some reason she'd never quite believed him. Instead she felt that there were things he didn't want to share with her, just as she did not want to tell him about her longing to lose herself in the arms of Kyle Dayton, if only for one utterly insane night of love.

John rose from the logs and with his back to her, started for the trailer without another glance her way.

"Wait!" Gillian called. "I'll tell you, okay?" Her hands had gone clammy. "I want to leave early because there's someone here in Weed Junction I don't want to see again."

John paused in his tracks and looked impatiently over his shoulder, demanding more.

"He's not just any man, you see. He's a—this big movie star. And I feel...awkward...around him."

Now John turned completely, his interest aroused. "What's this guy's name?"

Gillian would never have taken John Proudfeather as being star-struck. "Kyle Dayton."

She hadn't expected him to know the name, but at the mention, his eyes lighted up, one brow arched, and he said in his low, calm voice, "Kyle Dayton? Yup, he's big, all right."

"You know who he is?" She would never have guessed John had even set foot in a movie theater.

John nodded, lowering the lids of his eyes as he always did when he was thinking hard.

"So do you think you could help me out, John? In the morning? First thing after sunup?"

"Why not?" John said cheerily. "I can go for a walk anytime." And then, before there could be any more conversation, he disappeared into his trailer.

Gillian walked at a brisk pace, her spirits restored. She had set off to accomplish something on her own behalf and had managed to pull it off. Getting John Proudfeather to patch up the ailing Mustang wasn't exactly a monumental feat, worthy of a spread in *National Geographic*, but it was definitely a step, so to speak, in the right direction.

Gillian would ordinarily have taken the longer way home, going by way of the dirt road that led into Weed Junction. But tonight, because the moon was high and, in a sense, so was she, she felt brave and sure enough of herself to test her self-sufficiency further. She would attempt the shorter back way, an ill-marked route that zigzagged through the brush and trees lining the riverbank.

Starting off from John Proudfeather's, the river was located about a quarter mile to her left. In the moonlight, Gillian could tell the Rio Grande's exact location by the dark shape of trees lining the bank. Only here was the land surrounding Weed Junction verdant. In daylight the green reminded her of Vista del Bravo—the way it had been during the early days when she and Scott had met, fallen in love and shared the dream of preserving the natural beauty of the area from being developed into America's premier model community.

Yes, the vegetation by the river's edge reminded Gillian of Vista del Bravo before the bulldozers had torn away whole sides of rolling hills...and before Scott's ideals had similarly been eroded. He had fought her—his wife—in city hall, when she had marched up to the microphone before the council members to protest the destruction of an inland estuary—home to many wild birds—in order to build million-dollar back-bay estates.

That time, that awful moment in Gillian's life, had been the single occasion when she had been propelled to fight for something she believed in. Sick to her stomach, her legs turned into water, her mind so fragmented by fear that she could hardly remember her name, she had nevertheless spoken out.

Her stand had ended in personal disaster, of course.

And her relationship with Scott had begun so well! That was always the mystery of it, and what made her so frightened of being so unbelievably wrong about a man again.

When she and Scott had met, she had been a graduate student at the University of California. She was studying cultural anthropology, working on a Ph.D., after having already received Master of Arts degrees in sociology and psychology. What it had boiled down to was that she was very interested in people—on paper. That is, she was terrified of dealing with others on a one-to-one basis in the real world. It was far more comfortable to continue studying and collecting degrees, relating to the human condition on a theoretical level in textbooks, and in statistics gleaned from her perpetual field studies.

She had met Scott while she was working as an intern on the topic of urban societal structures. Scott worked for the city of Vista del Bravo. As a senior planner he was assigned as her temporary boss. Then he'd become her lover—and finally her permanent human connection, one that later turned out to be not so permanent, after all.

During their courtship, their mutual vision of building a suburban utopia had been the cornerstone of their relationship. Their love was new and unspoiled, and so was Vista del Bravo, the future site of the paradise they were to help form.

The new city of Vista del Bravo, once a Spanish land grant, was a vast landholding filled with orange groves and rolling green hills, beyond which stretched a coastline of pale sand beaches that opened up to the Pacific Ocean.

The plan was that Vista del Bravo would retain its environmental integrity and at the same time incorporate dwellings and businesses into the landscape. Man and nature in perfect balance.

It had taken exactly five years for the blight of human greed to set in.

Gillian had watched the orange groves go, tree by tree, acre by acre. In the place of greenery appeared rows of mock-Spanish stuccoed houses, mostly lookalikes. The people also looked alike. Everyone had blond hair and blue eyes. The kids all wore braces. Tennis suits and jogging togs were worn like a second skin. The promised "ethnic mix" was only in the automobiles the Bravarians—as Gillian had come to call them—drove to their surf and turf restaurants. Like their homes, arranged in neat rows, their cars would be lined up by cute, tanned parking-lot valets: Mercedeses, BMWs, Porsches, Ferraris, an occasional stodgy Rolls Royce, and perhaps a loaded-with-extras Japanese sports model.

As Gillian saw it, when the hills of Vista del Bravo had started going, so had her marriage to Scott. For Scott had seemed not to notice the carnage perpetrated by the bulldozers. When he did notice, he seemed to be in agreement.

So while she quietly swamped the city council with long reports attesting to the deleterious environmental and social ramifications of the exploitation of Vista del Bravo, Scott had maneuvered himself into ever more politically advantageous positions within the

city's bureaucratic hierarchy. Of course, right along-
side him had been Debby. But only with the benefit of
hindsight could Gillian insert that piece of the puzzle.

So by the time she made her scandalous grandstand
play to save the back bay for the birds, Scott had risen
to the position of senior planning director. Everyone
knew that it was he who had given the project that she
had hoped to block the green light, and that she was
his wife.

Clearly she hadn't saved the birds, nor had her stand
on behalf of the winged creatures done her marriage
any favors. Two weeks later it had ended.

And her history was precisely the reason that she
could not trust herself to be attracted to another male
animal who might again annihilate her emotionally.
Having by her own contrivance just circumvented that
distinct possibility, she was feeling very good as she
swung through the brush lining the route of the Rio
Grande.

Maybe she had been walking five minutes while her
mind had plunged backward into the miserable period of her life, a time she wanted to forget, yet found
herself drawn to just the same. The terrain had become more densely thicketed, and Gillian had to pick
her way carefully along the path.

The trail she was on curved inward toward the river's bank, and Gillian followed its course, moving into
the greenery that grew with lush abandon near the
water. Her shorts caught on a bramble, and she had to
stop and work the material free of the thorns. It was
strangely quiet as she worked; not even insects chat-
tered. Shafts of moonlight descended like arrows
through the branches of the nearest trees.

From somewhere near an owl called, its voice strident and unexpected in the expansive quiet. A rustle followed, furtive and rapid.

Gillian looked up. But there was nothing, only the breeze passing through the still world. Suddenly, the shadows took to dancing.

Captivated by the moment, Gillian absorbed her surroundings. Never had she been out alone at night in the wilderness. Waves of enchantment rose within her as she looked about, thirstily drinking in secrets kept from those who moved only through the world of sunlight.

Passages from her anthropology textbooks came back to her. To the Indians, nothing in nature was as the white man saw it. Their world was filled with sacred meaning. A leaf, a feather, the striations on a rock, all of nature was extraordinary and open to deeper interpretation. One only had to have the eyes to see, the heart to know.

She thought of the owl.

Once when they had been sitting outside his trailer, John Proudfeather had told her that the owl was the eagle of the night. As the eagle ruled the day, so did the owl have dominion over the night. Both served as communicators, bringing messages from other planes.

Around her, more phantom arrows dropped as the leaves of birch trees shivered.

Then once again the world fell still. Freed from the thistles, Gillian moved along the silvery path, carefully picking her way through grasses and shrubs that looked like blown crystal.

The owl cried again.

By now she was close to the water's edge, and the river's rushing kept up a background murmur to her thoughts. The earth beneath her sandals felt loamy and porous, and twice she slipped on a moss-slick slab of stone. Had the moon not been high and full, she would have been in trouble.

Then suddenly, just as she came through a tight thicket, the moon was no longer full. Instead it had become a slightly jagged crescent embroidered on the enormous, black velvet sky.

Somewhere nearby there was the crackle of brush. An animal, Gillian thought, looking to the right where the sound had originated. But for an instant the landscape was further obscured by a cloud passing before the moon, and all Gillian saw was the fuzzy outline of a small knoll with a single tree.

In the next second the clouds had passed, and the moon reclaimed the landscape, which now included a giant owl. The apparition stood on the top of the small knoll—a bird the size of a fully grown man, a creature that could not possibly exist.

Gillian blinked, looked again, and there it still was.

Up to now she had been too surprised to feel any fear.

But now the giant owl that couldn't be but was, turned and saw her.

For a second, she and it faced each other, staring as if neither of them knew what the other might be.

Then, before another second had elapsed, Gillian turned in the direction of Weed Juction and began a frantic dash along the river bank.

She didn't see the fallen log.

Her right leg hit it, the left became entangled in a vine, and she was off balance, falling. She was scratching at the earth, when a large hand grasped her elbow.

Chapter Five

It was not the incredible giant owl that had hold of her arm. It was worse than that.

"Are you okay?" Kyle Dayton asked, leaning over her, his voice sounding surprisingly stiff and emotionally removed for a man who had come to rescue a fallen damsel.

"Yes, yes...fine, thank you very much," Gillian replied in an equally formal tone that would have sounded better in an English drawing room. She cast a furtive look to one side—no owl. Of course no monster owl; how could there be?

She had twisted her body around in order to see Kyle and to make herself appear slightly more graceful. Now they faced each other at an angle, and she was concentrating very hard on not making direct, meaningful eye contact. But even so, the place where

his hand connected with her arm throbbed, setting off
a ribbonlike response of acutely tantalizing sensa-
tions throughout the rest of her body. She remembered the earlier moment when she had stood in her
bedroom, holding her breath, hoping he would knock,
fearing he would knock, and then being both disappointed and relieved when he didn't.

Kyle tugged gently and offered his hand, which
Gillian took. "Can you make it?" he asked as he drew
her to her feet.

"Thanks," Gillian replied, upright again. "Thank
you very much." She made a big deal of brushing
herself off.

"No problem. Glad I happened to be in the neighborhood." He too, stomped his boots and jeans free
of some riverbank vegetation and fiddled around with
the sleeve of his blue and green plaid shirt, which had
come unrolled from the elbow. A couple of times he
glanced her way, and she saw him take a breath, then
swallow—an impulse to add something more to his
last remark? she wondered.

Gillian, finished with her own busy task of remov-
ing leaves from her shorts, finally said, "Yes. Really.
Lucky for me."

For the sake of doing something new, she looked
down the bank into the dark waters of the Rio Grande.
Here and there, white froth glistened in the moonlight.

"You're all right?" Kyle asked.

Gillian saw his eyes searching for signs of physical
damage. As they swept her body—from yellow T-shirt
to denim cutoffs and down the length of her legs to the
tips of her sandaled toes—he might just as well have

been brushing his fingers over her, such was the remarkable effect of his gray-eyed, gold-flecked interest.

God help her, thought Gillian with a rush of panic, she was melting. She was becoming a puddle of emotion and desire and longing for this movie-star stranger.

"Fine. I'm fine. Great," Gillian assured him calmly. She waved her arms in a little display of physical fitness. "See, no harm done ... all's intact."

"It looked like you took a pretty bad spill," he commented.

"Did it?" she asked lightly.

"Yeah ... bad." He followed his statement with a solemn nod.

"Not that bad, really," Gillian said. "I'm pretty agile. And tough," she added.

At her last remark, a subtle change of expression appeared in Kyle's eyes, and accompanying the mysterious tinge of seriousness, his brows furrowed, knitting together toward the bridge of his straight, elegant movie-star nose. "A woman alone—out here at night? You think it's safe?"

Gillian didn't reply at once. Here was Kyle Dayton standing before her, looking handsome and concerned and solid, and she wanted so desperately to rush into his arms and say, "Yes, yes ... everything hurts me! My whole self hurts. And I don't really know you, but I'd like to. I want to hold you and have you hold me, and it's been so long since anyone has acted as though they really and truly cared about me...."

Instead she settled for, "Sure, it's safe out here," accompanied by a self-confident smile. The fearsome, two-legged owl was only a figment of her imagination, some trick of the light. It was a tree caught in a shadow, nothing more. "Anyway, like I said, I'm a tough city girl."

"Regular Roller Derby material." He returned her smile.

She hated that. His smiles weakened her. And the idea that he might be able to see past her carefully boarded shutters smacked dangerously of intimacy. The territory was already far too treacherous. Here were moonlight and water and soft earth to lie upon. Here were a man and a woman....

The words slipped out like actors polished in their roles who had been waiting in the wings. "The truth is, if it hadn't been for you, I wouldn't have been out here in the first place."

Kyle's face was a blur.

"I was afraid of getting involved with you," she said. "That is, I sensed this...well, this attraction. So I went over to John Proudfeather's to see if I could talk him into taking a look at the Mustang first thing in the morning. That way I wouldn't have to be with you again."

When she had finished, she heard silence ringing in her ears, silence as loud as a siren, paradoxical though that was, and she knew she had just done something really, really stupid for which she would kick herself all the way back to Los Angeles. How could she have thought that honesty was the right tactic to employ? A rising tide of humiliation rose hotly up her torso, attacking her neck with prickles of shame.

Kyle was no longer a blur; unfortunately, he had come back into sharp focus, and she was being pinned by the potent gray eyes.

"No kidding," Kyle said.

Then he began to smile, and then—to Gillian's horror—he was laughing.

The laughter hit her like cold water dashed in her face.

Gillian stared at him, despising herself for being such an incredible jerk, and wanting to punish him for recognizing it.

There was nothing she could say. It had all been said, and this hilarity was the result. It was what she had wanted, so she should be glad. Her body was entirely safe now.

She turned on her heel, and almost tripping over the log again, saved herself with a little skipping jog, and went rushing down the path, seeking the route to oblivion.

When she got to her hotel room, she sat down on the edge of the bed and stared at herself in the mirror across the room. She took in her stricken expression. Truth was always bitter, she recalled.

For the second time that night, Kyle found himself standing before the door bearing the #2, his fist poised in midair.

On the opposite side of the door Gillian listened. She sat with her back against her headboard, her knees pulled up. Tears hadn't come. She had thought they would, had waited for them, but when they didn't, she supposed that was just a sign that there weren't any left after crying so much over Scott.

She had heard Kyle's footsteps coming down the hallway. She knew it was Kyle, because there weren't any other guests in the hotel. His boots had made hard, masculine, self-assured sounds on the plank flooring, and in her mind she could see him exactly as he was: hard, masculine and self-assured. She had his image memorized—green and blue plaid cotton shirt, sleeves rolled carelessly to the elbows, the colors blending to perfection with the gray eyes fringed in black lashes. She saw the stone-washed jeans hugging the muscular thighs, and the hard, tanned chest showing just above the third button down... with shoulders that were...oh, God...

For a moment Kyle continued to stare at the door. Thoughts moved across his mind like heavy furniture being pushed from one place to another. But no matter how he arranged it, the woman did not fit anywhere into the vast scheme of his life.

Kyle put his hand down. And yet he did not move.

At eye level, the #2 continued to glitter like treasure waiting to be plundered.

But he didn't want to hurt this woman.

Earlier in the evening he had thought about making love to her—or at least having sex. The "love" part had been more of an idealistic flight of fancy.

What if he had told her that he was lonely as hell, and even if it meant just pretending for one night, he would have liked to feel close to her? What if he had told her that the reason he had been out walking along the riverbank was because he was trying to exercise lust out of his loins?

She probably would have laughed in his face.

What she had said was that she found him attractive and that she was afraid she was going to be used because he was a handsome, famous movie star. It was true. If they did sleep together, the next day she would get into her car and he would get into his, and that would be it. Technically it would be another one-night stand. Not because either of them necessarily wanted it to be that way. What they both wanted—if he had any insight at all—was the same thing, a caring relationship with some genuine closeness. But for whatever reasons they were both afraid, both too damaged to be able to make life turn out any differently for themselves than it had in the past. And besides, look how they had met. He was heading in one direction, and she was going in the other. If nothing else, that fact should make things pretty clear about the future.

Kyle turned away from the #2's invitation, and made it back to the safe refuge of the less intimate #3, whose face, he noted, was somewhat tarnished and not as brilliant as that of its neighbor. Or maybe he just saw it that way.

Back in his room he showered, dried himself off, slipped into bed and shut off his mind. The talent to shut down his mind was another benefit he had picked up as a kid, when the pain of waiting for his mother to return, as she had promised, got too great to bear. In less than five minutes after hitting the mattress, Kyle was asleep.

Gillian was not as fortunate. Her thoughts did not race; they stagnated, fixed on the reality that only a minute ago, Kyle had stopped by her door, paused, and moved on to his room. She wasn't even worth a sexual ravishing.

Her life was no more than a desert wasteland, as dry and parched, Gillian realized, lying on her back and staring at the ceiling, as the landscape beyond the window of her room. Emotionally, intellectually and financially, she was turning into human terrain as dried up, hopeless and lifeless as the Sahara. Finally, hot tears began to stream slowly and silently down her face.

The knocking was very faint at first. It seemed to be in sync with the rhythm of her heartbeat. The sound was obviously another figment of her imagination, just as the owl had been.

Only it wasn't. The rapping against her door was absolutely real, increasing in volume even as she grabbed the sheet from her bed and rushed across the floor to fling open the door.

Kyle and she stared at each other from either side of the portal. He had on his jeans, his belt undone, the silver buckle dangling loose as if he had flown into his pants and shot right out the door. He didn't even have on a shirt. She could make out the definitions of smooth muscles. Gillian swallowed and pulled the sheet tighter around her body, feeling faint with a rush of dread and desire.

It was dark, but light enough from the moonlight to read the ripples of feelings passing across Kyle's face. There was struggle. There was masculine passion.

For a second neither of them said anything. At the same time they both made tiny throat-clearing noises and started to say something. And at the same time they both stopped.

Then, before Gillian could think further of what to do or say, Kyle had stepped across the threshold and had taken her into his arms. His eyes burned into her, searching her face, and with a breath that was more of a cry, he pressed his lips against hers.

Gillian felt herself locked within a hot orange flame.

She didn't know who she was anymore. All she knew was the touch of his fingers on the side of her face, the hand pressed against the small of her back, the hot, wet feel of his lips moving lower to the hollow of her collarbone, trailing kisses to the rise of her breasts just above the sheet.

Burning, she felt the coolness of air against her bare flesh as Kyle unwrapped the sheet. The cotton fell with a glad whisper of release to the floor.

A brief flash of sanity possessed her. "Kyle... no...."

"Yes... yes..." he said, and it was too late for any other protest. With one fluid movement he closed the door behind them, twisting the lock against the rest of the world.

His gaze traveled the length of her unclothed body and lingered, as if unwilling to let the vision go. Then he was reaching for her, once more meeting her eyes with his own as he backed her against the door.

Closing her eyes now, Gillian gave in to his exploration, her hands roughing the thickness of his hair as he moved his mouth from breast to breast, feeling with his fingers for the fullness of her flesh. Within her, fire raced along strings that joined her nipples to an apex of pleasure.

She had never known... never known... never....

Arching against his mouth, she could feel the heat of his breath against her pelvis, sense the quickening of his desire for her. Matching it with her own, she urged him lower with her hands.

The pressure of his tongue made her tremble, setting off miniexplosions within her. He knew what she was feeling and teased her on and on, stopping just as she felt herself climbing to where light met darkness, where the world stopped and another universe opened.

"God...oh, God..." she gasped, consumed with need for him. "Kyle...yes, please...."

She was trembling, her legs barely able to hold her, her body a shivering flame. She was electrified. She could not endure.

But she did.

Kyle pulled her down to him. On her knees, she faced him. His tongue owned her mouth, the fever from his explorations blocking all thought from her mind as with one hand on her breast, he led her fingers between their bodies and closed her palm over himself.

She began, but he stopped her. She began again, this time making him shiver and cry out in exquisite torment, and again he held her still. "Not this way...not yet...oh, God...!" Kyle was moaning now, his voice low and fierce. He made a motion to lift her, as if to carry her to the bed, but instead his hunger ruled, and he pushed her gently but urgently to the floor. With their eyes open to each other, he drove himself into her. It was molten silk. It was a river of pleasure. Joy...it was joy.

"Gillian..." Kyle spoke her name in a half gasp, stopping, his arms trembling with tension as he poised himself above her, holding himself still, then slowly reentered her. Again and again he moved—and stopped just as they were ready.

She thought she would not be able to stand the pleasure, that surely the explosions of light that sizzled against the dark landscape of her mind would increase until she was burned up by the energy, reduced to sheer feeling. She was losing herself, and it didn't matter.

Kyle's face tightened, his neck muscles growing taut, his eyes holding her until the last second when he lost himself, too. Now their contact took on another dimension as Gillian rode the light, bursting into flame, climbing higher.

She heard the echo of her cry. It was her voice, but she could barely recognize it.

Then, coming down from where she had been, from the place Kyle had taken her, she realized she was no longer the same.

She had been touched; she had been altered. She had broken into a million pieces. There were feelings, subtle and mysterious feelings she had never known before.

Tears. There were tears in her eyes, tears rolling down her cheeks. She began to cry softly, so softly that only her own heart could hear.

"What . . . what . . . ?"

Worried and soft and tender and masculine, the voice was sweet like honey.

Kyle had raised himself on one elbow. He was looking into her eyes, examining her face. Seeing the

tears, he lifted a finger to brush them away. Somehow he understood.

Gillian knew she wasn't alone anymore. Kyle had
entered her heart.

Chapter Six

He was there with the crazy big bird—an owl or something like it—and there was Gillian, who was in danger of being... what? What was happening to Gillian? He had to help her. He was...

Awake. Kyle opened his eyes, and the knowledge that he had been dreaming seeped into his mind, just as the light from the window began to infiltrate his retina.

But it took a while for the panicky feeling that had overtaken him in the dream to subside. At the same time, memories from the night before began to move in. Suddenly he was fully awake, a happy wildness shoving aside all other impressions. Gillian! Beside him. Gillian!

With a sigh of satisfied completeness, he turned his face into the other pillow, at the same time reaching out with reckless joy to draw her back into the crook of his arm where she had lain the last hours.

Only she was gone.

Kyle sat up, at first listening for sounds hinting that she was in the bathroom. She wasn't. Nothing but a heavy silence filled the room. He ran his hands through his hair, prodding his mind to come up with something to explain her absence.

Disappointed, he got up and slipped into his clothes, noticing as he did that hers were, of course, gone.

Well, he would probably find her downstairs chatting with Stella, who he knew would be as curious as hell to hear about what it was like to make love with a major motion picture star. And he knew Stella would know they had slept together. Stella was the kind of woman who knew things, especially the deepest and darkest of secrets, without ever having to be told outright.

Or maybe, Kyle thought, Gillian had simply become hungry and had gone looking for some breakfast. She was being considerate, not wanting to wake him. That was it—she had been hungry. In fact he was hungry too. He'd find her, and they'd have coffee together, maybe eggs or pancakes and bacon, ham, biscuits. God...he hadn't felt like breakfast in years. But this morning was different. Yes, very different. And so was he. He was happy.

He even looked happy, he thought with pleased amazement, noting his expression in the mirror as he used his fingers to smooth his hair into order. He couldn't wait to see Gillian.

As he walked down the stairs, the notion that he was happy continued, growing in him like a delicate bubble, a happy, light bubble with colors of the rainbow reflected in it. He was maybe even a little in love.

In love? He, Kyle Dayton...in love? He tried the notion on for size.

Yes, it fitted; he was a little in love. The impossible had happened at long last. And the bubble in him became lighter and more colorful, and his steps grew faster as he ran down the last few stairs to the lobby.

"Seen Gillian?" he asked Stella, who was working on something on top of the check-in counter. She was wearing a short white and black and red Japanese happi coat. Two chopsticks pierced her hair, which she had bunched into a tight ball on top of her head. Kyle saw she was already fully made up, eye shadow, rouge, the works.

Stella looked up. Kyle had expected to be met with a collusive, lecherous smile. Instead, Stella seemed disturbed by his question, and then, quickly looking down, she said in the begrudging tone of someone forced into a betrayal, "Gillian's gone."

At first Kyle thought he hadn't heard her right. He couldn't have, because it didn't make any sense that Gillian would have left him. So he waited, thinking Stella would add something to what he had heard.

Stella raised dark, clouded eyes, and with a sigh said, "I'm sorry."

And that was when he fully understood. *"Of course Mummy's going to come back for her little guy. Mummy loves her Kylie sooo much."* She had rubbed her nose playfully against his. *"So don't you cry now. You just watch for me out that window."*

Gillian was gone.

With the realization came a wave of misery. It touched everything, drawing him under. To save himself, he had to say something, had to move, but he was unable to get free of the gloom.

Suddenly a violent emotion consumed him, and he swung around, smashing his fist into the thick adobe wall with the force and determination of a steel wrecking ball. The impact hurt like hell, and the pain felt good. It was clean and honest and something tangible that he could deal with. And yet in the next instant he felt himself dying again, just as he had so many years ago, when he'd known for certain that there was no reason to keep up his vigil by the window.

"I'm sorry..." he heard Stella say behind him. "I think she wanted to stay, but she—"

"Yeah, sure, sure..." Kyle said, turning, but unable to look at Stella as he made his way to the front door. He had really made a jerk of himself with the histrionics. Inside he was still shaking, but still, he was an actor, so he made his voice jaunty to accompany his careless shrug. "Yeah, she had to go—"

"—had to leave," Stella finished, her words overlapping his.

At that he did turn to look at Stella. He laughed and shook his head. "Yeah," he said again, rocking back on his heels, "I know how that is. When someone's got to go, they just gotta go."

Breakfast was being served at the Kachina Kantina, and Kyle forced himself to order eggs and pancakes and bacon and coffee and orange juice. Just as he had planned, but minus the other party. He tried to eat it, but there wasn't any sense in trying. He was dead inside. So he sat there. He sat with his eggs and pancakes and felt like crying, but of course he couldn't, because thirty-two years later, he was still being brave. Besides, he was the number one movie star in America and had everything in the world to be happy about.

John Proudfeather came up from under the hood of the Mustang and straightened. He might be old, but age hardly seemed to affect his stature or bearing. At the moment he was eyeing Gillian with that same strange look she'd noticed the night before when he'd caught her lying. Only now she hadn't said a thing. Maybe he expected her to lie.

"So?" she asked, sending a glance toward the Mustang.

He nodded.

"Does that mean . . . ?"

John nodded again.

"It's okay? Wow. You really fixed it. No tow truck, no new engine?"

John closed the hood firmly. It was still early, barely seven-thirty, and not hot enough for him to burn his hands on what would become scorching metal within the next three hours.

"Well, that's great, really great," Gillian said, realizing that her tone didn't exactly match the statement. "So, uh, what was it, anyway? The thing that was wrong." And the moment she said "wrong," her eyes flickered down the road in the direction of Weed Junction. And Kyle.

"Clogged fuel line is all," John said in a low, uninterested monotone.

Gillian looked back to John, but a part of her mind was still traveling. Kyle would probably still be asleep. Or maybe not. Maybe by now he would have woken up and discovered she was gone. Would he care?

Probably it would be no big deal. Ha! He was probably glad she had left. She had saved him from having to make up some stupid little speech about how it had been grand and all, and they'd have to do it again sometime, and it really meant a whole big bunch to him, her being so unique among the thousands of women he'd known. And...oh...here was his card, anyway, so she could call him sometime, but of course he was going to be in Madrid or Madagascar or on the moon or something, so maybe it would be a while before they could get together again.

Her troubled eyes had lost their focus. When she suddenly came to, John Proudfeather was looking at her with his pinpoint stare. She could feel the pull of his thoughts.

"What?" she said.

"I didn't say anything."

"No? Oh."

"That'll be fifteen bucks," John said abruptly.

"Oh, sure...of course." She fished around in her wallet, brought out the cash and handed it to him. "Thanks, thanks a lot. I really appreciate you coming out so early. A station would have probably really socked it to me. I'd be stuck with a new battery and well, who knows...a whole new engine or something...."

John nodded.

"Well, thanks again." Gillian started edging herself toward the driver's door, feeling he expected something more of her, but not knowing what. "And . . . good luck, John."

John nodded yet again, and Gillian imagined she read a flicker of amused disdain in the dark eyes.

She got into the Mustang and it started right up, just as John had said it would. She gave him a thumbs-up sign, and he nodded again without a word or a smile. A minute later, as she picked up speed, taking the road out of Weed Junction for the second time in two days, she glanced into her rearview mirror. John was a small speck in the distance. But the red shirt stood out against the landscape, and she saw he was moving fast into the desert as if he had something important to do.

Then she decided it was bad luck to look back.

Hadn't she looked back yesterday, and hadn't things ended in disaster? She would keep her mind clear and her eyes turned forward. Kyle Dayton was history. From here on in, everything was going to be just fine.

A few more feet down the road she couldn't help herself; she had to take one more last look into the mirror. It was a quick look, but even so, the view brought back a lot of memories. Each one stabbed again at her heart.

There was nothing there anymore, just a trail of yellow dust settling into the tracks the Mustang left, and which the wind would soon blow away. And in no time at all it would be as though nothing had ever happened, as if she had never been there.

Suddenly she couldn't take it anymore. She slammed her foot onto the brake pedal and did an abrupt U-turn. Dust rose in a bilious cloud as the car sped back toward Weed Junction.

* * *

At the bar, Kyle paid for his totally untouched breakfast. Even reaching into his pocket seemed an effort. To breathe was labor. His thoughts moved in slow motion. Before this morning, when he wasn't feeling particularly buoyant about life he would think of *Due West* to make himself feel better. If he continued to think about *Due West* and the effect his film would have on a lot of little boys in theaters across America, he could actually forget himself. But this morning nothing could fill the hollowness within him.

Kyle thanked the bartender, who was also the waiter and the cook, and turned to leave.

At the same time the door swung open, and a cowboy entered. His spurs made clinking sounds as he walked, just as they did in the movies. Kyle gave him a little nod as they passed, and pressed his hand against the top of one of the swinging doors, pushing at it.

It didn't budge.

Someone else was coming through, and Kyle stepped back, giving the next guy room.

It wasn't a guy.

Immobilized by shock and disbelief, Kyle could only stand where he was.

"Hi," Gillian said softly. She looked embarrassed, even uncertain as to how she happened to be in his company.

"Hi," he said flatly.

A crazy gladness had seized him. Movie stars didn't act uncool around women—it was a law of the universe, probably written in fine print somewhere in his contracts—but he wanted to lift her up and swing her around in his arms.

The sun was behind her. The lighting made her face appear pale, so that the hazel eyes were all the more pronounced. If he forgot about the cutoffs and yellow top, she might have stepped from a Renaissance painting. The memory of how she had looked and sounded and tasted last night intruded, and he pushed the thoughts away before he found himself utterly undone by her radiance.

"Stella said you'd be here, so I thought..." Gillian stopped, looked down, looked back up and said hesitatingly, "Kyle, I—"

"Had to take off. Yeah. Yeah, I know. Stella told me." He added dryly, "What would we do without Stella? Maybe we'd have to talk or something."

It was strange, but suddenly he wasn't glad to see her anymore. The initial rush of gladness had turned into something else. Shifting his weight, he took a step forward, as if about to leave. But he didn't. Instead, acting as though the thought had just struck him, he said offhandedly, "Hey, you ought to try the pancakes here. Terrific stuff. Oh, but you probably know that already, don't you?" He looked down at her, and it required hard work not to be affected by the eyes, wet now, although he could see she was trying hard not to show her feelings. He had hurt her. The good side of him wanted to comfort her; the other side wasn't going for it. Why should he bother? Coming back was due to some second thought she'd had. What he had felt for her last night deserved more than a lousy second thought.

"You have a good trip back to L.A...." That was all he said, and then he was moving past her into the morning sunlight.

He kept on walking, listening for her voice to call out for him to stop. But she didn't.

The cowboy had tethered a pinto to an old iron stake in front of the Kachina Kantina, and across the street, parked in front of the Weed Junction hotel, was the Mustang. Kyle squinted at the rattletrap. A tender, protective feeling filled him. It took all his willpower not to turn around and see if she was watching him.

But there was nothing to talk about. He wasn't going to be a fool about this. Between the ages of five and eight he had been fool enough for any man in one lifetime—waiting for a woman, trusting a woman.

He passed through the front door of the hotel. Fortunately, the lobby was empty. He wasn't up to making small talk with the effervescent Stella Sanchez.

Gillian stood frozen in the darkened bar, then forced herself to leave. All the terrible feelings of rejection she had experienced when Scott left her seemed to gather together, reassembling themselves for a grand, triumphant curtain call. Her marriage had been nothing. And this was nothing—at least not to Kyle Dayton.

She walked across the street, eyes kept to the ground. She wondered if he was in his room. Was he watching her now from his window? Maybe she wasn't even important enough to warrant a curious glance. She couldn't look, couldn't break down.

Keeping her mind on the Mustang, her eyes on the handle, she wrenched open the door, and was suddenly spun around by the shoulders.

"Why the hell did you run out on me?" There was fury in the words. Kyle's eyes blazed.

"I—I didn't!"

"No? That so, huh? Then how is it that I woke up this morning wanting to hold you—"

"It was me! Oh, God, it was me. I was running out on me!"

"Great defense, really great...." Kyle's jaw was rigid, his coloring ashen beneath the tan.

He still had her by the shoulders, and Gillian could feel the degree of his anger in his grip.

"I guess it wasn't right...I just didn't think...." The stalled tears flew from her eyes. "I'm sorry, but—"

"Not even a goodbye, dammit! A note? A telephone number, an address?"

They were shouting, and in the vast stillness their voices resounded with the power of cannon fire.

Then all at once they were folded into the silence of the country. They gazed at each other, Kyle with his arms hanging at his sides—Gillian across from him, feeling defeated, her face wet with tears that clung stubbornly to her skin.

Kyle's chest rose and fell. He made as if to say something more, then after a false start began again, speaking haltingly. "Look, last night you made a speech—"

"I'm sorry about that. I'm sorry that I said those things," Gillian rushed to say.

"Well, it seems you're sorry about a lot of stuff this morning. Anyway, you don't have to be sorry about the speech. I liked it."

"Sure, I'll bet. Who wouldn't want that kind of flattery? And you've probably heard it a couple of million times."

"I never heard it at all. At least not put that way. Other people don't tell the truth."

"And for good reason." Gillian followed the statement with a small, bitter laugh, which Kyle chose to ignore.

"The thing is, I don't always tell the truth either."

Gillian felt her insides twisting. Now he was going to tell her that last night was a lie. He was going to say it outright, and then she could feel *really* rotten.

"Look, spare me the gruesome details. I don't want to hear it, okay? Honesty's never done me too much good in my life. And anyway, I already know the score, you know? You were a great actor, splendid performance, really, really top-notch, Academy Award material...and I was a terrific audience for you, lost myself totally in the drama. But now everything's cool." She took hold of the car's door handle again, and was about to slip onto the seat when she was yanked up and pressed against Kyle. His eyes were hot flares of anger, and somehow he seemed to have grown taller.

"Are you through?"

"Yes. Absolutely. Finished. So to speak." She tried to pull away. Kyle held tight.

"I'm *not*." And roughly he brought her chin up and kissed her hard on the lips.

It was a long kiss, the longest, most potent, most heartfelt, searching, yearning, smoldering, desperate and knowledgeable kiss in the world—or so it seemed to Gillian, who when finally released, thought all her bones had been removed. She could barely stand, much less concentrate on formulating a verbal response.

"That's the truth," Kyle said. "That. So, now that you know, the rest's up to you. Stay or go. You know where I am."

With that he turned and went into the hotel. From outside she could hear his boots on the stairs to the second floor.

Her gaze moved upward to the second story of the Weed Junction Hotel and hovered at the window of Kyle's room. *It was up to her.* Gillian brought her eyes down and took in the solid terrain of Weed Junction. Beyond the hotel there were no more than a few squat adobe buildings, and half of those had their windows boarded. There was the post office, which was actually part of a home that was part of a store that sold fishing tackle, soft drinks, beef jerky and oil lanterns, plus a host of other unexpected and unrelated items. And there was the adobe house occupied by Billy Riggs and Carrie, with a large sign hanging at a slant over the door, saying Rock Sale. A few other of the local inhabitants also sold goods from their houses, opening up the doors and hanging out their signs like flypaper whenever a tourist made a wrong turn and wandered into the time warp of Weed Junction.

It was up to her.

Gillian's attention shifted back to the hotel, from which the sound of Linda Ronstadt could suddenly be heard wafting through the window of Stella's apartment. And then Stella's voice joined in, all but drowning out Linda. Stella. That Stella. She sure lived life. Even in Weed Junction, where there was hardly any life to live, Stella managed to turn boredom into the stuff of grand opera.

From the window, Linda and Stella continued to wail passionately about a man, their voices rising and falling, crying and sailing along through the empty spaces of a town that was supposed to have been called Glory. Moving toward the source of the sounds and glancing up at the window of Kyle Dayton's room, Gillian knew she was in big, big trouble.

Chapter Seven

It happened on the third day they were together in Weed Junction. Gillian was called on to make another decision, one far more important—and terrifying—than the last, when she had merely been required to venture up the stairs of the hotel and knock on Kyle's door.

Kyle had answered immediately, as if he had been waiting with his hand on the knob.

The emotion in his face had made it easy for Gillian to fall into his arms. He'd held her close against him, not saying anything, but keeping her there as if afraid she was not entirely real and might dissolve at any minute.

And, in truth, for the past two days her life had taken on all the elements of a storybook existence.

She and Kyle were like two children, ecstatic in each other's company. They played, they talked, they laughed constantly, and sometimes their relationship took on a silent delight, as each discovered in the other the feelings and visions experienced by themselves.

But in spite of her happiness, Gillian could not be completely at ease. There was always that feeling that at any moment she could step onto a land mine, and the whole illusion would blow up in her face. The happier she became, the more pronounced was her sense of impending doom.

Then in the midst of her anxiety attacks they would make love, and the doubts would be momentarily assuaged. Even she had to admit that they fitted together, body and soul.

"Truck's fixed. It's downstairs. Stella signed for it," Kyle announced, putting down the phone as Gillian came out of the shower with a towel around her. They had just made love, and Kyle still lay unclothed in bed, a sheen of moisture on his perfect leading man's body. "I've got wheels. Life can roll again!" He raised both arms above his head, like a fighter signifying triumph.

"Great," Gillian said, "great." She flashed a quick smile, then turned to reenter the bathroom, where she could be alone to work through the news about the truck.

The room was still steamy, and her face was only a blur in the clouded mirror as she leaned against the sink for support, wondering if this was going to be the end of it. It had taken this long—two days—for the station in Santa Fe to repair the truck. Kyle had insisted on keeping it, rather than getting another rental. So basically, as she had known all along, he'd really had no choice but to remain in Weed Junction. In that case she might have been deluding herself into thinking she was anything more to him than a pleasurable convenience.

She started as Kyle appeared in the doorway.

He had slipped into his jeans, but was otherwise undressed. "Hey," he said, bringing a hand to her chin and drawing her face around, "what's going on?"

"Nothing," she said, her tone lacking conviction.

"Something..." He waited. "Tell me."

She shook her head. If he was exiting her life, she didn't want to make a scene out of it and spoil the good that they had shared. The time had been magical, more than she could ever have hoped for. But if it was over, then it was over, and she should just be glad of having had the experience.

As she looked into the gray depths of his remarkable eyes, she felt she had come a long way in the two days they had been together—had matured emotionally—because she could actually say without her voice wavering, "So the vacation's over, I guess."

"It's over, yes."

Gillian's heart constricted. He had said it so easily. Still, she remained outwardly unmoved. Anyway, Kyle seemed not to be seeing her. Her courage was wasted. To judge by his expression, his mind roamed elsewhere, making plans for the future, she supposed, plans that would never include her.

Then he was back with her, his gray eyes measuring her body with masculine approval as he leaned against the door frame. "Come on," he said, "get dressed before I'm tempted to stay in bed with you all day. Let's do today up right."

"Last day of vacation," Gillian said, smiling bravely. "Remember when we were kids at school, how special that day seemed?"

Kyle said, "Yeah, special." He turned abruptly, as if to cut off the subject, and went back into the bedroom. "Hungry?" he called. Now his voice sounded normal again.

No, she wasn't hungry. She was miserable and didn't think she would ever want to touch food again in her whole life. Better that she waste away to bone and end the misery she was already experiencing. With every passing second, the notion that this was their last day together became more real.

"A little," Gillian lied.

"Pancakes," Kyle's voice boomed from the other room. "I could handle two orders on my own."

He did eat an order and a half of the Kachina Kantina's special beer batter pancakes, while Gillian picked at two fried eggs, sunny-side up. The yolks appeared to be huge orange eyes staring up at her with mockery.

Afterward Kyle helped her into the truck. He seemed almost elated, whistling to himself as he started the engine. Now and then he would take her fingers into his hands and bring them to his lips, kissing them. But his mind seemed mostly elsewhere as they drove along the road that passed out of Weed Junction in the opposite direction to the main highway.

It was getting increasingly difficult for Gillian to keep up her facade of composure. She wanted to scream at him to at least have the decency to appear mildly depressed over their parting.

Kyle stopped the truck when they had wound along a rutted path leading into the desert and up a gentle elevation. "Come on," he said, jumping from his side and opening her door.

They walked together, Kyle not reaching for her hand as at other times. He seemed preoccupied, as he had during the drive.

"Look," he said, and pointed into the distance, "over there." It was a medium-sized butte, a flat-topped land mass jutting out of the desert terrain. A few scrawny stalks of some hardy vegetation clung to the reddish earth. Otherwise the formation of sand and rock was barren.

In five minutes they had reached the bottom of the rise, and it took a couple of minutes more to climb to the top. A wind had come up, and its intermittent gusts whipped at the yellow sundress Gillian had put on to look especially good on their last day together. It was cut low, with a formfitting bodice that followed the line of her body to below her hips, where the skirt expanded into soft folds. It had been a long time since Gillian had cared how she looked, but today was important to her. She would remember everything about this day, and she wanted Kyle to remember her as being beautiful and desirable.

At the top, Kyle strode around the rim of the butte, while she watched him take in the panorama of desert and mountains and the gleaming thread of the Rio Grande in the far distance. From one side of the ridge they could see the scattered buildings of Weed Junction, appearing like pieces of a tiny, toy village such as

those used in model train layouts. As he looked down
at the spectacular view, Kyle's face bore the excitement of a small boy.

"This is it," he said softly to himself. "This is it,"
he repeated, turning to Gillian, who moved to take his
outstretched hand. He scooped her against him so that
they both looked out to the same horizon of sunlight
and towering white clouds. "It's perfect. It's *Due West*
exactly."

And holding her to himself, he told her the dream.
Gillian pictured it unfolding before them. She felt the
story's passion and identified with the heartache and
the triumph, both of the lone man against evil and of
the woman who stood beside him to the end. He spoke
of the grandeur of the land, of how it was sacred and
that there was in every man an obligation to care for
its well-being, for it, too, was a living thing with a
heart. As the words passed his lips, there was the throb
of music in his voice, and in the wind blowing against
their bodies, Gillian imagined the sounds of an invisible orchestra rising and falling with the film's emotion.

Then Kyle was finished, and the only sound was that
of the wind blowing across the huge empty territory.
His arms were wrapped around her waist as she leaned
against him, holding her hands over his. He kissed the
top of her head.

"Well?" he asked, and waited for her response.

"You'll have a hit," she said softly.

"Will I have you with me?" Kyle asked.

Gillian was afraid to move, afraid she had been
mistaken.

"I'm going to need a technical advisor for the historical accents. You'd be perfect. We see everything the same. We'd be a fantastic team."

Gillian pulled away, suddenly attacked by a wave of nausea. "No," she said violently.

"Gillian . . . ?"

"No," she repeated, but without the force. She turned to face him. "I'm going to go back to L.A. I have a thesis to write."

"You said you don't even have a topic—"

"I'll get one."

"No," Kyle said, stepping forward. She backed away and he stopped, as if not to terrify a wild animal. "What's wrong . . . what's this all about? You're afraid, but I don't see why. It would just be for a couple of months at the most, and the pay would be good. You said you loved it here . . . and . . ." He hesitated. "And I thought you felt something for me."

"Oh, God . . ." Gillian cried, and whirled around so that she didn't have to see his face. Nor could he see the torment she was experiencing. "It's too much like before," she said in a soft voice. "I told you about Scott . . . about how we had this grand vision. And then it all went wrong. The vision, the relationship. I don't want to get into the same situation all over again."

"I'm not Scott," Kyle said evenly. "And there aren't any bad guys out to tear down hills and plant houses here. Gillian, it's a chance for us to be together. We can get to know each other better. And we can really do something good together—just as you wanted to in Vista del Bravo."

The words were soothing, and as Kyle spoke, a better picture of the future formed in Gillian's mind, one that was rosy and not black. Everything he said was true. It was an entirely different situation. And she did care for Kyle. Care for him? That was slightly understating the facts. She adored him. She worshiped him. Yes, and she loved him already.

"I won't let you down," Kyle said.

Gillian looked into his face and saw that he meant it. But she had to ask anyway, just for the record. "Promise me?"

"I promise not to let you down."

There was a long silence, then Gillian said, "Kyle, I lied before. I'm not really so tough."

"I'm not going to disappoint you," he said. "We'll have great shots of the land out here, and we'll make people want to keep the environment as it is, pure and healthy. A lot of little kids are going to see it, and they'll remember, and when they're grown, they'll care the way we do."

"I care so much, Kyle..." Gillian said, her voice choking, as the tears that she had managed to hold back all day began to fall freely. "I care about *you*."

And then they were together again, he was holding her, and Gillian felt the wind and sun on her skin.

Kyle closed his eyes. He brushed his face against her hair, and tenderly raising her chin, brought his lips to hers. He tasted a tear, and something in him broke. Love came shining through him for this woman he had grown to love so intensely in such a short time.

He would never let her down.

Chapter Eight

Like a circus coming to town, they came to Weed Junction. They pulled down the main street in trucks and vans and motor homes and cars drawing trailers. Amid the dust and heat of mid-August came laughter and music and sharp, irreverent explosions of disbelief when they first sighted the place that would be home to most of them for the next two months. And of course there were the expressions of awe for the surrounding scenery.

First to arrive was the technical crew. This included carpenters and grips and cameramen, wardrobe and makeup and hair professionals, setting up their own small provinces amid Kyle's larger kingdom, all in accordance with his precise instructions.

Gillian was truly amazed at the range of Kyle's expertise. The man who made intense love to her each night, whose body sometimes seemed to her a combination of liquid fire and the sweetest honey, who gently cradled her in his arms until dawn, had other sides to him that she would never have believed existed.

Once, before she knew him, she had thought he was nothing more than a pretty face and an ingratiating personality. How wrong that was. He knew every aspect of the film business from the bottom to the top. And because *Due West* was severely underfinanced, he found it necessary to troubleshoot in almost every area, rather than call in additional expert assistance.

With wings seemingly on his heels, Kyle flew from one place to the next, giving this man a pep talk, lambasting another, appearing to know everything that was happening and caring deeply about the slightest detail.

No, thought Gillian, she had definitely not made a mistake. This time she was right on the mark: Kyle was through and through the man she had dreamed he was, the man she had wished Scott had been. Kyle was genuinely honorable. What you saw was what you got.

But busy as he was, he never lost track of her. She would be perched on a stool, leafing through an old historical journal she had borrowed from the museum in Santa Fe to check some element of the set for authenticity, when Kyle would suddenly appear and sweep her into his arms, kissing her passionately. He didn't care who saw—and everyone did. He was in love. And so was she. She didn't even care what others thought—probably that this was just a movie-location romance. It wasn't. This was the real stuff.

Along with everything else, Kyle was playing the lead role, which he confessed was not his original intent. Producing and directing were work enough. He had wanted to get Robert Redford for the hero's part. He knew Redford would agree with the film's scope and intention. Unfortunately, he couldn't afford Redford or anyone else in that league, so to guarantee a showing at the box office, Kyle had to stick his own name over the marquee.

When the other actors joined the crew, Gillian saw faces of top character players, actors she had always respected. "People who care about their art and about what they're representing to the public," Kyle had told her proudly. When he said it, the words resonated in her heart. He would often say things like that, and it was as if he had pulled out her own thoughts, her own feelings.

There were many times when her heart was so full that she couldn't even find words to speak. She would just stare dumbly at Kyle from across an expanse of desert as he set up a scene with a cameraman, and when she happened to catch his eye, he would stop for an instant, take in her expression and smile, nodding to her because, even separated, they could feel the other's thoughts.

Yes, this was the real thing.

A brilliant young actress—Constance Aiken—had been hired to play the leading lady's part. Her hair was a natural flame red, and her eyes as green as a South Sea lagoon. Kyle said she had agreed to do the part for next to nothing, taking a percentage of the box office net instead. She wanted the part for what it said, and she believed in Kyle's ability to bring in a blockbuster film. If Constance hadn't have come with her husband, a handsome sculptor, and their two young children, Gillian supposed she wouldn't have slept nights for worrying that Kyle might find himself smitten.

And along with the members of the cast and crew, other people straggled down the road to Weed Junction. Some of these onlookers came from nearby, where word had spread that Kyle was filming. Others came from a lot farther away, from neighboring states and even from as far away as New York. Kyle, the legend, was packing them in.

For the most part Kyle allowed the visitors to gape, as long as they didn't interfere with the filming.

Of course, Stella and Carrie wriggled into any scene where a woman was needed as background. As for Billy Riggs, well, it had been three weeks, and he still hadn't returned. Being securely in love herself, Gillian had, for a nice change, emotional energy to devote to the personal misfortunes of others. Stella said this was the longest time Billy had ever been gone, and said outright that things didn't look particularly good. As for Carrie, she tried to put on a show of not caring, but occasionally a red nose and puffy eyelids would testify to the contrary.

As for the local Indians, a few of them showed up to see if there would be work as extras, and some sold their jewelry and rugs and pots. Kyle hired a handful of the native Americans as background for some special scenes, but this wasn't a Cecil B. deMille production. There was a lot of story, a lot of beautiful scenery, but not a lot of people.

Gillian thought John Proudfeather would have made himself more visible, but in fact he only appeared now and then, sometimes alone and at other times with the two elderly squaws.

"John," Gillian said one day when she saw him, "I thought you were a big Kyle Dayton fan. But you hardly ever show your face."

John nodded, saying nothing, as was usually the case unless he was after something. He started off, then suddenly turned back to her. "You don't have that scene right—that one with the little house down by the river." And then he told her why in detail. She in turn told Kyle, and Kyle thanked John personally, making the necessary changes in accordance with John's input.

And periodically this continued to be the case: John would appear to tell Gillian that something or other needed correcting if *Due West* was aiming for authenticity. The strange thing was, she never really saw John watching.

One moonlit night when she and Kyle were out walking, they took the path back to the river. They were speaking of the day's filming, when Kyle suddenly stopped and held Gillian still, placing a tense hand on her arm.

"What?" she whispered.

"Wait...wait...." And then Kyle said, "Look...."

Gillian followed Kyle's nod to what appeared to be a knoll, and recognized it right away as the place where she had been terrified by the vision of the big owl.

For a moment she saw nothing, and then—there it was! The giant bird! Again. It had suddenly hopped into view from lower down on the small hill, and was clearly visible now as it moved slowly about, raising and lowering feathered arms as if doing some sort of dance.

Kyle and Gillian exchanged looks of disbelief.

"It's not real," Kyle said.

"It's not. It's just...the light," Gillian affirmed doubtfully.

"Not the light—it's a man. Come on," Kyle said, and they ran at full speed toward the knoll.

But the giant feathered dancer disappeared from their view. By the time they reached the mound, there was no sign of him, neither visually nor audibly. He—or it—had vanished into the night.

"I saw it that night when I fell down by the river," Gillian admitted. Winded, she and Kyle had collapsed onto the ground. "It's a little embarrassing, but I thought the thing was real at first. I thought I was going crazy."

"It is real," Kyle reminded her, then laughed.

"Real strange." Gillian giggled. "That's why I was running, you know. I was escaping from it." She waved her arms up and down, mimicking the bird-man.

"I was afraid, too," Kyle said, suddenly growing more serious as he appeared to think back to that earlier night. "It's why I suggested it wasn't entirely safe out here after dark. And it isn't."

"Oh, come on. It's just a...an owlie. An owlie! Get it?" And Gillian toppled over, laughing so hard that she had to hold her sides. It wasn't that funny. She knew it wasn't that funny, but when Kyle looked down at her, shaking his head, she had to laugh even more. "Look at this. Owlie tracks." She pointed to vague footprints that were visible in the moonlight.

"Jogging shoes," Kyle said, and they looked at each other as understanding dawned.

"John?" Gillian suggested.

"Gotta be. He's practicing being an Indian, I guess."

Gillian nodded slowly. "Yeah, maybe so. Well, what do you know about that? Never too late, is it?" And she smiled slowly as she found a fallen feather lying beside her foot. Kyle stuck it by her ear.

It was early September, and the days were still hot. But changes were in the air. Subtle as they were, Gillian could feel the differences in each day, as if a wheel had slowly begun to turn. In the evenings the sun had begun to sink behind the mountains earlier, and on some of the higher peaks, white patches of snow glittered from the first tentative snowfalls.

Gillian remembered that not long ago she had stood outside the Weed Junction hotel and looked above to where the clouds ranged over the earth. She had considered that lofty place the location of heaven. But she was wrong. Heaven was here in the dirt of Weed Junction, and in the feeling of love that expanded within her heart each day she spent with Kyle. Some of those days were hard and long, and there was certainly a good selection of aggravations to endure. Even so, the love only grew.

"Autograph, Kyle? Name's Bob. Thanks, hey, thanks a lot. Loved your last movie. Hey, man, didja really make it with that blonde? She was hot, man!"

"Me, too. Please, Mr. Dayton. To Ginny. G-i-n-n-y."

And so it went, the daily ritual of filming and fans. Kyle was always good-natured, forever patient. It was

Gillian who sometimes found herself fidgeting, wishing the groupies wouldn't take up time with Kyle that she wanted for herself.

It was during one of these trials that Gillian noted the man at the edge of the crowd.

At first she thought he was someone's father, but after watching him a bit longer, the role didn't seem to fit.

Since by nature she was a watcher, content to live out her life on the sidelines, she had developed a certain skill in observation. And now, with nothing much else to do, she practiced her craft.

What she noted was that while she was watching him, the man was himself checking out everything and everyone else in the vicinity. But to Gillian his interest seemed different from the idle curiosity of a tourist. There was purpose in the blue eyes—an electric blue, she registered. The strong color veritably vibrated against the deeply tanned skin, which was further highlighted by a showy thatch of absolutely white hair.

Subtlety certainly was not this man's strong suit. Not only did he have white hair, he also sported a white Stetson hat, and fitting over his tall frame was an expensively tailored, two-toned beige and white cowboy suit. The only hint of bright color in his ensemble were the small insets of turquoise stones on his white hatband. Yet, despite all the white, Gillian found nothing angelic about him.

Only once did their eyes meet. The brief joining was awful.

It was as if she were a mouse sniffing around some cheese, when suddenly a trap slammed down on her. The grip of the man's gaze was every bit as lethal. Be-

hind the blue look, where the light of humanity
generally shone forth from other eyes, Gillian experienced only flat calculation.

The day was warm, but she felt a chill travel through
her bones as he turned away, moving on down the
street until he came to a white station wagon. Fasci-
nated and troubled, Gillian continued to watch as he
climbed in, repositioned his rearview mirror, and a
moment later headed out of town.

Later that night there was a massive barbecue,
compliments of Kyle, to celebrate the halfway mark of
the filming of *Due West*. The shindig was for the crew
and cast and anyone else who happened to be in Weed
Junction, and was held in the middle of the main
street. Long trestle tables had been set up, and chairs
were delivered from a rental company in Santa Fe. A
live cowboy band was performing on a small stage,
and Stella had already been up with them two or three
times, warbling several of Linda Ronstadt's hits while
she wiggled to the beat in a tight red dress, its rows of
black and red ruffles outlining the plunging bodice and
the bottom of the skirt.

She was on a break, doing serious work on a barbecue rib and gossiping between mouthfuls of beef,
when Gillian asked about the man in white.

"Yeah," Stella said, licking her fingers and wiping
them on a crumpled napkin. "I know who you
mean."

"Well?"

"I don't know. He's been here before. Just hangs
around, looking, you know, but I don't know who the
dude is."

"He gives me the creeps," Gillian said.

"Dresses nice, though."

"A tad flashy, perhaps?"

"That's what I mean—dresses nice." Stella pointed a rib at Gillian. "Have I told you you're looking a whole lot better these days? Didn't I tell you? I said a man would agree with you—put some color in your cheeks, stars in your eyes. Ah, love, love, love!" she exclaimed, and grabbed another rib.

Gillian left when a local rancher showed up to tell Stella she reminded him of Linda Ronstadt.

Kyle was nowhere to be found. For twenty minutes Gillian searched the party and even the perimeter, where Kyle might have gone to talk more quietly with someone about the film. She wondered if he had gone up to their room in the hotel, but there wasn't any light on. It was just by chance that a while later she happened to glance up at the exact moment the light was switched on, then a moment later off.

The door was locked. She tapped lightly, calling, "Kyle? Are you there? It's me."

At first there wasn't a response, then she heard rustling sounds, and finally the definite sound of Kyle's walk coming across the floorboards.

He had switched on the small reading lamp by the side of the bed. It was his own, sent from Los Angeles, and he used it at night when he didn't want to disturb Gillian's sleep. But now, even in the weak light cast by the small bulb, Gillian could see that something wasn't right with Kyle.

So she asked the obvious, knowing the biggest issue to Kyle was the movie. "Something's wrong with the filming?"

"Nothing," he said, moving back to the bed, where he sat down.

Gillian noted the rumpled pillow, where he must have been lying in the dark, thinking. And then, walking around the bed, she saw a manila file folder with papers scattered beside it. There were sheets with figures neatly inscribed, financial data related to the film.

Gillian looked down at him. "Money problems? You're running short?"

Kyle looked up. But there was a veil over his eyes as he said, "No. I have everything I need to finish the film."

"And get it distributed?" Gillian asked, having acquainted herself with the various steps of the movie business.

"And get it distributed," Kyle said. "Gillian, this isn't your business. Just drop it, okay?"

He had never done that before. He had never shut himself off from her, and that he did so now came over both as a shock and a familiar sensation. Scott had always closed down on her.

Old hurts and new fears confused her. For a moment she merely stood where she was, silently looking at Kyle, who was gathering together the scattered sheets of financial data. Then, not knowing what else to say, she said only, "Sorry," mostly because she was very, very sorry, and left the room.

Chapter Nine

Kyle wasn't asleep when the door opened close to midnight. There wasn't much of a moon out, but even so, the window brought in enough light so that he could see Gillian as she felt her way carefully through the room. She undressed slowly, now and then looking his way. There was no chance she could tell he was awake behind his lidded eyes. And that was good. He didn't want to have to speak with her, for then he would be forced to lie.

With all his being he wanted to touch her. Never did her beauty fail to excite him, and now, looking at the darkened silhouette, she appeared to him even lovelier and more desirable than ever. But what he felt was far more than sexual energy seeking release; he sought closeness of being, the communion they'd reached with just a touch and a smile. It would be hard to smile now, impossible.

A minute passed, during which his thoughts continued to tumble in agonizing turmoil, and then she returned from the bathroom. Lightly she slipped into bed next to him. He could feel her eyes seek him out, her glance touching his face, and knew that there would be hurt and questioning in their mysterious, foresty color. There was the now familiar warmth of her body beside him, only inches away, and he knew also that she would be wanting to touch him as much as he wished to hold her. The mingling of the smell of soap, of the faint scent of perfume, even of the desert air on her person, was too much for him to bear, and it took all his willpower not to reach for her. Had it been any other night, they would have spoken for a while, trading stories on the day's events, and then they would have made love.

But he had no right to do that tonight—not anymore, and God help him, perhaps never again. Not after what had happened today.

When he thought back on it, it wasn't the first time he had seen the man. Some days before he had noticed him, mostly because of his striking appearance. At the time Kyle had thought he was just another one of the people who hung around, checking out the movie scene. But the man wasn't a tourist, not by any means—although he had certainly been checking things out.

This afternoon Kyle had found out why.

His production assistant had handed Kyle a business card. It was expensive and refined: white linen finish with black embossed lettering. There was no company listed, only the man's name: Dirk Baylor. No phone number or address had been included.

"This guy wants to talk to you," the assistant said. "He said to tell you he's not just a fan. It's legit business."

Kyle studied the card for a moment. Looking up, he said, "Tell Mr. Baylor I've got a movie to make. At present, that's my business. My only business. If he wants to hang around, we can talk around lunchtime. But I'm not making promises, either. I might be tied up at lunch, too. Tell him that."

As it happened, Kyle found himself free to see Baylor. Gillian was busy anyway, unable to join him as she was talking to John Proudfeather, who had happened by with some advice he deemed critical to the production.

They began the meeting with a handshake.

"Wanna grab a bite?" Kyle offered. "Chow's on the house."

Baylor accepted, and they picked up some fried chicken and salad from the catered spread put out for the cast and crew, then took their plates to a quiet spot at the side of one of the real houses. Some false fronts to mark other buildings had been inserted for filming purposes. Kyle and Dirk Baylor balanced themselves on a couple of rickety old chairs, using a small table for their drinks. Baylor, in his pristine white and beige suit, looked out of place, but not entirely. In his pseudo-dude-cowboy garb, Kyle could imagine him a hundred years back, a dandy cardsharper, maybe; a man with a pearl-handled fast gun.

"So what's our business?" Kyle asked, chewing on a drumstick.

"You might call it commercial development."

"Yeah? What might *you* call it?" Kyle asked, looking sideways at the man in white.

The blue eyes narrowed. "Me . . . I'd call it a necessity."

Kyle nodded, giving himself time to fill in some of the blanks. "Interesting term, necessity. Would you care to be more specific?"

"As specific as I can be," Baylor said, adding, "under the circumstances." He fingered a drumstick, twirling it between two fingers, and again Kyle thought of a pearl-handled pistol. "Some people—some interested parties—from the capital sent me here on their behalf."

"Washington?"

Baylor laughed. "Local. Santa Fe."

"And what do these interested parties want?"

"Money. They want to make some money. You see, they think its real good what you're doing here, filming *Due West*. Very promising enterprise is how they see it. They're big admirers of your work."

"Is that a fact? I've got fans in high places, huh?"

They had been chatting casually so far, but now Baylor's voice changed, turning flat and cold. The blue eyes hardened as they met Kyle's semiamused expression. "I presume, Mr. Dayton, being from Hollywood and the business being what it is there, you haven't just recently fallen off the turnip cart. So I'll be brief and to the point."

Kyle waited. Baylor dropped the piece of chicken onto his plate and stood up. He carefully wiped his fingers on a napkin as he moved a few feet from where

Kyle sat. He spoke to Kyle in profile, all the time, looking out to the mountains.

"These men who sent me to talk to you—they want to capitalize on the good work you're doing here in Weed Junction. They're visionaries, to put it in more poetic terms. They see there's a good opportunity to turn this area into a major tourist attraction. What they're banking on—literally—is that after *Due West* comes out and is the big hit it's sure to be, then a whole lot of people are going to be interested in seeing where all the action took place. The way they figure, all these people coming out here are going to need hotels and shops and roadside restaurants, maybe one of those wax museums showing Indians and desperadoes, and a whole lot of other tourist attractions. And they also figure that a road, a good paved road that looks like it's leading somewhere, and not just this dirt driveway that takes people to Weed Junction now, would be an added incentive to visit the area."

Kyle didn't say anything. It was clear enough who was scheduled to lay out the funds for the road.

"And what's going to make me want to pay for their road?"

"They'd like to think of it as a gracious contribution." Baylor smiled slightly. "Oh, but there's another little detail of their request." He moved to face Kyle directly. "They think it would be an added asset if some of the false fronts you've put up for your shoot will be turned into the real thing."

"They want a real road and they want real buildings."

"Excellent. You understand."

"What's to make me want to spend my money on all of this?"

"It's not a question of wanting. It's a matter of necessity, as I said before. You'll find it imperative that you go along with the program. Because some of these gentlemen have it in their jurisdiction—I don't like to use the term power, as it smacks too much of violence—to see that your permits for filming here are pulled. There could be all kinds of environmental flap. And you wouldn't want that, would you?"

It was hard for Kyle to remain cool, but he knew it was in his best interest to do so. He needed to get information on who his foes were and on the extent of their capability to follow through on their threats. "I could fight it."

"Sure you could," Baylor said. "That's the American way. But by the time you fight it, you're going to be out of money. You can't keep this crew and cast just sitting around while the wheels of justice grind slowly, can you? You have contracts to honor with them—paychecks to sign." Baylor took a few steps closer. He looked down at his boots and scowled slightly. The decorative, lizard-skin finish was coated with fine dust. He brought up one leg at a time and brushed away at the buff-colored hide. With both feet on the ground again, he studied the results of his work and said, "So, I don't think there's much to think about, is there?" He looked sharply at Kyle.

Kyle stared back, but he was seeing Gillian, hearing her voice the night she told him about how Scott had let her down. Except for the time and place and face, this would be history repeating itself. *If* he acquiesced to the demands being made by Baylor. But how could he not do what they wanted? Baylor had been right about his position right down the line. Kyle had gone into filming the only way he could—on a shoestring budget. He'd been strapped for time and capital from the outset. Because of his health record, he hadn't even been able to purchase delay insurance.

"Actually I've got a lot to think about," Kyle said, returning his attention to Baylor.

A vein on Baylor's temple gave a slight jump, of surprised agitation? "Hope you think fast."

Kyle rose, too. He and Baylor were both tall men, evenly matched. Baylor was older and broader, the extra weight he carried appearing solid, not giving any evidence of a softening middle-aged spread. He started off, but Kyle held back, stooping to pick up the paper plates and cups.

"An environmentalist, huh?" Baylor commented wryly, turning to wait.

"Yeah," Kyle said, "I think it's important to keep garbage off the face of the earth. All kinds." And he stepped up his pace, leaving Baylor behind.

That had been this afternoon. But tonight Baylor and his demands were very much with Kyle. The words spoken between them lay in his bed, separating him from the woman he loved.

"It was John," Gillian said to Kyle the next day, when they took lunch together. They sat alone together at a small table off to the side of the longer trestle tables, where the others dined.

In the morning she and Kyle had arisen, made polite and stilted conversation, both obviously aware that anything they could say would only escalate the tension that already existed. It was the first morning they had not made love. A brief and perfunctory kiss had been their only physical contact as they parted ways for their respective duties.

"What?"

"John—it was John Proudfeather who was playing Big Bird out there near the river."

"Was it?" Kyle answered absently. He held a sour-dough roll in his hand, but it hadn't been bitten into, and it appeared that he didn't even know it was there.

Gillian looked down, concentrating on moving pieces of lettuce around her plate with her fork. "You're not here, Kyle." She looked up again. "You're not listening to me, and you're cutting me out, and..." Her voice grew soft and almost child-like. "It frightens me."

"Gillian," he said, a heavy dullness in his voice, "don't be frightened. There's nothing to..." He broke off with a sigh.

"There," she said, hurt. "You're doing it again. There's something wrong. You say it's nothing, as if it's my imagination. But I can feel it. I can tell, Kyle."

"Look, it's nothing. I'm thinking about the film, nothing major, just little odds and ends, and my mind gets distracted. So," he said, attempting to add enthusiasm to his tone, "what did John say? Why's he dressing up as a bird?"

She didn't really want to talk about John now, but since it seemed their only immediate point of contact, she went with the option Kyle had presented. "It's an experiment, he said. He didn't really want to discuss it." She held back from adding the obvious "either."

"But you pried it out of him anyway," Kyle said with a smile. He even put some butter on his roll.

"As it happens—yes. I did. It seems that John became a little interested in his own heritage. All my questions about his tribe must have gotten to him. He said—in a very low-key way, mind you—that he started to remember things. Like how his grandfather used to talk to some of the spirits. And his father, too. John didn't say it outright, but they must have been medicine men."

"A family thing, like lawyers? Or banking families and doctors?"

"Yeah, witch doctors."

They both laughed. The laugh was an instant bond, and when their smiles faded, Kyle said, "I love you. I love you, Gillian." And he reached across and took her hand, squeezing it as if to impress his feeling.

"I know you do," Gillian said. "That's why I don't understand . . . why I know there's something. . . ."

Kyle removed his hand. The spell that had joined them was broken again.

"Just trust me," he said after a beat.

"I do trust you. Is there some reason why I shouldn't?"

The question hung in the air.

"I've got to get back to the set," Kyle said, and pushed himself up from the table.

"But you didn't eat anything!"

They both stared at the plate for a moment, as if examining a crucial point of evidence.

"I'm not hungry—too much coffee this morning, I guess."

And then he was walking away, leaving behind a trail of questions.

The afternoon was taken up by work, both she and Kyle busy with their own tasks. At dinner they barely spoke, partly due to the tension between them, and also because Kyle had—for the first time—invited the leading lady and her husband to join them, ostensibly to discuss some of the finer points of her characterization. It was entirely obvious to each of them that the splendid young actress needed no coaching, and the entire dinner was a dragged-out affair, a miserable sham.

Kyle again ate very little. Gillian noted that fact, along with a hundred other signs. Her eyes were constantly occupied, searching, gathering small details, hunting for clues as to what might possibly be the cause of the sudden rift in their previously idyllic relationship.

What she came up with was exactly nothing. Nothing had occurred between them to cause him to back off in this sudden manner. And from what she could discern from the shooting schedule, location gossip, and from watching the daily rushes, *Due West* was evolving in the best possible way.

So it had to be something else.

Naturally, the idea that another woman had entered Kyle's life came to mind. When she thought back on the unraveling of her marriage to Scott, she saw how stupid she had been not to recognize the signs of his infatuation, and later of his physical involvement with Debby.

Ordinarily her very last idea of the cause of Kyle's sudden disaffection would have been interest in another woman. But what did she really know? Kyle was a famous and handsome movie star. Maybe he did this sort of thing all the time.

That night, the worst happened.

"Hi!" Gillian said, turning from the dresser, where she had just placed some fresh laundry.

"Hi," Kyle returned, casting a quick smile her way as he entered the hotel room. He left the door ajar.

Gillian passed him and closed it.

Kyle, who had gone to the briefcase that lay by the side of the bed, turned as he heard the door click shut. "I'm going out again," he said.

"Oh." Her heart gave a slight jump. She told herself not to react. He was going out, but maybe that meant that he had to give someone a piece of paper— look, even now, he was reaching for a manila folder— and he'd tell her he'd be back in five minutes. And then they would talk and laugh, and tonight they would make love, and everything would be . . .

"I may be late tonight," he said, standing and holding the folder with both hands, as if it were something precious he was afraid he might drop.

"Very?" Gillian asked, her throat tight. Her heart was beating very fast, and she felt as if she might become hysterical and make a terrible fool of herself. Then she would certainly be lost—a fool in Kyle's eyes!

"Maybe." He moved past her, going toward the door. With his hand on the knob he stopped, and with his head hanging slightly said, "Probably. There's a lot to—"

"Well, just don't tire yourself out," she said, sounding to herself like some idiot, some maternal jerk. He was half out the door when she called, "I'll wait up for you!"

He stopped. "No...don't. Just get some sleep."

"Kyle!" She could see him tense. He knew, he knew. None of this was her imagination. There was something dreadfully wrong. "Can't we...can't we talk?" She was pleading, but she didn't care.

"I've got to go...."

And he did.

The next morning, so did she. Kyle had come back into the room late—almost three. He smelled of beer. Rather than undress, he merely lay on the bed, fully clothed but for his boots. She didn't dare touch him. She didn't know what to say. In fact she didn't know who he was anymore. The man she had loved only three days before was no longer in this stranger's body.

She drifted off to sleep sometime before dawn and awoke just as the door of the hotel's room closed. Gillian checked the time on Kyle's digital clock-radio. It wasn't six yet.

If she didn't take some sort of action, she would certainly do something desperately unfortunate. She couldn't bear to be around him and not be a part of his world—which she obviously wasn't anymore. He was incredibly busy, totally involved with his film. From the sidelines, where he could not observe her watching him, Gillian examined his interactions with others. He smiled, slapped backs, spoke ingratiatingly, joked on occasion. It was only when their paths crossed that she felt him stiffen and turn into the stranger.

"I'm going into Santa Fe," she told him, stopping by as he was coming down from one of the camera dollies after setting an angle.

He gave her a sharp glance. "Santa Fe?"

"Yes. I thought I'd meet with that historian—the one I told you about who was an expert in old customs. We've got the dining scene coming up, and I thought maybe he'd have some little bit of business to make it look especially real."

Kyle was staring at her, through her. "Yeah, that could be good." Then his eyes cleared and he was seeing her. "What time do you think you'll be back?"

For a moment the question spread joy through her. He still cared! But then she cautioned herself that he might be asking merely to make sure that he wasn't around—or worse, involved with someone when she returned.

"I don't know... probably by dinner."

He nodded. "Well, drive carefully. Are you taking the Mustang?"

"Yes. I thought I would."

He nodded again. She waited a minute, thinking that he would say something more, deliver some fragment of hope for her to carry with her down the desert highway. Instead he touched her lightly on her arm and gave her what was a small appeasing pat, the way one would dismiss a child with affectionate but basically disinterested regard, before setting off to deal with another chore.

The sound man was saying something about the mike picking up too much of the background noise. Kyle knew it was a significant problem that needed to be settled, but the words were entering his head as no more than a stream of mushy syllables running together; his eyes followed the blue Mustang that was pulling out of town.

There was an instant when he felt panic rise within him, and he had to restrain himself from tearing after her in his truck. It felt as if he were losing her, as if he had already lost her. But then he told himself that he was being foolish, that he was merely reacting to the psychological symbolism of the car pulling away, that he was no longer five years old and that this was a different woman. Gillian would return to him. Gillian and he would work things out. All he needed was a little time to think of how to deal with the Santa Fe situation.

"...if we position it by the wagons," the sound man was saying as the Mustang faded from view.

"Yeah, that's good, it'll work," Kyle said, turning back with an effort. "Let's do it."

And he walked off, dizzy with worry, to tackle a new problem concerning a stunt to be performed the next day, when a band of desperadoes was to come shooting through town.

In Santa Fe, Gillian met with Dr. Pauling, a small and tremendously enthusiastic man who spoke rapidly about infinitesimal facts until Gillian, who was generally intrigued by little-known historical details, found herself straining to remain awake.

After two hours of Dr. Pauling's breathless monologue, Gillian gathered together her notes and expressed her thanks for the invaluable history lesson. Dr. Pauling insisted she call him for any additional help. He knew everyone as well as everything, he assured her cheerily, his weak brown eyes alight behind thick glasses.

It was late afternoon when Gillian turned off the highway onto the dirt road leading back to Weed Junction.

Her mind had been filled with Kyle on the drive to Santa Fe and back. In her head she had run through any number of possible scenarios of how to deal with him. She could just let things take their natural course; she could present him with an ultimatum—either they talk about what had happened to cause the change in him and thereby the alteration in their relationship, or…Oh, God…could she do it? Could she even *think* such a thing? She would leave and return to Los Angeles.

Lost in thought, she was surprised by a pickup truck that pulled out from the side of the road and almost hit her. She braked suddenly, barely avoiding the other vehicle, which passed by slowly, as if they hadn't been a hairbreadth from a collision. The driver and passenger, both men, leered and laughed at her. In response, Gillian pounced on her horn, sounding her own feelings.

She noted, but did not take particular heed of the sign affixed to the side of the truck: Cabe Brothers Engineering and Survey Company. In the back she saw a couple of tripods and various other items of equipment related to land survey work. She had a momentary flashback to similar trucks coming off the hills of Vista del Bravo, hills that had later been ravaged and torn by bulldozers and dynamite, after a visit of survey teams such as the one she had just seen.

Dusk was settling onto the plain as she came into town. There was only a little activity in the street; it was too early yet for dinner. Mostly people would be resting. She parked the car and got out, looking, as she did so, up to the window of the hotel room she and Kyle shared. It was dark.

Chapter Ten

Kyle put on a good show; after all, wasn't that his profession?

After the day's filming he had joined some of the others at the Kachina Kantina. He downed a few beers and exchanged some old war stories of other location shoots, keeping his easy manner in place until, in spite of himself, his ability to dissociate gave out and emotions too potent to be buried threatened to explode the social facade. The smile that had made him famous slipped from his face. For a while he didn't even know it until someone made a comment.

"Hey, Señor Doom . . . hey dude, *qué pasa?*"

What *was* happening? If only he knew.

He tried to pick it up, to coast along on the others' high energy. Punch lines came in rapid fire from the group of seasoned wits, but this was humor lost on him. He continually lost the drift of the jokes; he laughed too early, or not at all. Floundering in mid-sentence, he would pause and take a drink, trying to remember what he had begun to say. It was no use; the knack of social pretense had deserted him.

It wasn't hard to dissolve from the scene. He merely drifted out of range slowly, talking to this one, slapping the back of the next, putting some change into the old-fashioned jukebox, and in a minute he had made his escape.

Outside, he stood for a moment on the cantina's boardwalk. The laughter and music were faint in the background as he stared at the darkened hotel window of the room he and Gillian had shared for the past few weeks. Gillian... just her name sent an ache tearing through him.

He was afraid, no, more than afraid; he was almost paralyzed with anguish. He could see everything falling apart and didn't know what to do. The idea of losing Gillian...

Joy. Remarkably, joy had come to him. It was something he hadn't counted on in his life, and when it had arrived—long overdue—it had come subtly, gradually, disguised in a hundred different forms—a night of lovemaking with a beautiful woman, a walk beneath a dancing sun at midday, a dinner of chili and beer served on a wobbly table in a café that wouldn't rate even a half star. These were the masks joy had worn before he recognized its true face in one woman, in Gillian—his life, his love, his breath, his very soul. His Gillian.

William Shakespeare had written for posterity that it was better to have loved and lost, than never to have loved at all. Rot, William. The very threat of love lost was looking to him more like an endless and unendurable hell.

Any move he made would cancel out happiness. If he didn't squeeze out the funds for the road and buildings—hard to do, but he had discovered after having gone over the figures last night that it was possible—he would lose every cent he had in the world. The nameless men from Santa Fe would pull his permits to shoot on location, and there wasn't enough money to start over somewhere else. His dream of sending *Due West* into the world would collapse. And if he did go along with their program, then he would lose Gillian.

The realization propelled him off the boardwalk and down the street, walking somewhere and not knowing where. He only knew that he had to move into this land, a territory that was either to be his salvation or destruction.

He well knew the shape of the future. In no time at all the serenity would be broken. Hoards of tourists would come eager-eyed to see an artificial rendition of the Old West. There were scores of these places in California and Nevada. Weed Junction would be plumped up, painted, and pushed into a hundred different commercial shapes, its soul imprinted with the stamps of twenty different credit cards. The earth would be scraped and dug and paved to make room for the campers and trucks and vans and cars. Signs hawking hot dogs and malts would take the place of clear space, and rather than tumbleweed, wrappers of candy bars would fly through the air. No one would hear the wind's voice anymore.

It was becoming dark, but Kyle kept walking, seeking the silence and solitude of the land and perhaps hoping for its friendship while there was still time. He could not help but feel his connection to the earth beneath his feet, and hated the power of destruction that had come to him unsought.

Without a plan in mind, he found himself going in the direction of the Rio Grande toward the spot where he and Gillian had come together in their funny and touching encounter, each wanting the other, both fighting their needs.

The sky dulled to a misty rose color as the last of the afternoon's light died away, settling behind the mountains. It was good he was wearing a pullover, for the air had taken on a chill. The season was definitely changing. Some leaves had fallen and made crisping noises beneath his Tony Lamas. He was glad that he had come. There was peace here. He smelled water and earth, leaves, and from somewhere not far off, the clean, brisk scent of piñon wood being burned.

He had only walked fifty feet more when he saw smoke drifting in cloudy patches across his path.

Looking to his left toward Owl Knoll—as he and Gillian had come to call the rise in the earth, Kyle saw three forms silhouetted against the last tint of rose-colored sky, three forms gathered around a dying fire.

Kyle stopped, taking in the vision of John Proud-feather, Maria and Pablita swaying back and forth to the sound of John's low humming. Or was it a soft, lowing chant? he wondered.

Kyle hadn't been there for more than forty seconds when the ceremony came to a sudden end, as John rose and doused the fire with dirt. The two women did not wait, but moved off silently together, taking themselves down the other side of the knoll and disappearing from Kyle's view. Only John remained.

Kyle was torn between curiosity and the need to walk alone, to keep his own counsel. It was John who made the decision for him.

The Indian came down the hill, walking with purpose toward Kyle, as if he had broken up the fire ceremony for that very reason. He moved with an agile grace more befitting a younger man, thought Kyle as he waited by the river's edge.

But even before John reached him, Kyle recognized the difference in the older man's eyes. There was an aliveness that had never appeared before; and when John came to stand a foot away, Kyle experienced a violent intensity of feeling.

"Sorry if I intruded," he said by way of opening. "I didn't mean to break things up back there." He sent a glance towards the knoll. "I was just out walking, passing by—"

"You can pass by, but I live here," John said brusquely. "Me and my friends, this is our home."

"Yeah, sure," Kyle said, trying to get behind the words to what John really meant. He didn't have to try hard. John made it clear in the next sentence.

"They sent some men out here today from Santa Fe."

Kyle stiffened.

"They're measuring the land for a road. They plan to put in a paved road—four lanes of paved road," John emphasized, "coming off the highway. And they're going to build some parking lots. After that, other men are coming out here. These men have big plans, too. Motels and hotels. Restaurants. Miniature golf," John said with a snort of disgust.

Kyle was stunned. He couldn't believe it. The bastards were moving ahead even before he had agreed. John was waiting, looking to him for answers. What answers? He couldn't say it wasn't so, because he didn't know what was going to happen.

"You brought this trouble here," John said vehemently.

At his words, the last rays of sunlight faded behind the distant hills. It seemed colder. And of course it was—they were suddenly no longer friends, but two adversaries wrapped in night, one man of light skin, weighted with the burden of executing a grim deed, the other a man of dark skin, charged with defending a rightful cause.

Kyle saw the theme as clearly as if it had been written out in treatment form for a movie deal. Only this was real—good against evil, man against nature. Hell. He didn't want to be the bad guy.

"Look, nothing's been decided yet," Kyle said truthfully. Even so, he heard guilt in his voice, along with the apology for what had not yet happened.

"Stop the movie. If you pull out, there won't be any reason for their stores and restaurants."

"I know. I know that."

"Then stop them," said John. "Get out of Weed Junction. Get off this land before they bring all their ugliness here like they've spread it everywhere else."

"Listen, I know how this looks, only there's more to it. It's not that simple—"

"It's simple. You stay. Or you go."

"I'm trying to tell you, walking out isn't all that easy. I've a lot of money invested in this movie."

"Money," John repeated.

The word sounded ugly, in Kyle's mind dripping with hellish images from a Hieronymus Bosch painting—souls writhing in torture. But this was undeserved guilt. His intentions were not evil; they had meant nothing but good.

"And it's a dream I had, too," Kyle defended himself, feeling as if he were bargaining for his soul. "I wanted to bring something good to people by making this film. That was my intent. I hadn't planned on these guys moving in on what I was doing. What's so damned ironic is that I wanted to uphold some values that were important to me when I was a kid. I wanted other kids to have something to hold onto, too. I'm not against you—I'm with you."

"What was the value? Money?"

"No, not money. That was the last thing on my agenda."

"What?"

"The land, of course, its beauty—the importance of keeping things as they are here," Kyle said wearily. "I hadn't planned on this happening, believe me."

"It's happened. So now you've got to stop it."

"I don't know if I can."

"You just get out. That'll stop it. And if you can't do that, then I'll stop it." John started off, moving over the dried leaves as silently as a ghost.

"Hey!" Kyle called after him.

The old Indian paused and looked over his shoulder.

"I don't know what you have in mind, but these men...I don't think they're kidding around. That's not how I read this. There's big money involved. And they're powerful, John."

"I have my own power," he answered.

"I'm sure you do, but—"

"I have my own power," John said again, then turned and became a part of the darkness, blending with the trees and shrubs and whatever else belonged to the land.

At the sound of the door opening, Gillian jerked her head up. Her heart lurched for an instant, then resumed its even beat, only faster than before as apprehension replaced her state of hopeless lethargy. But she didn't move from the bed where she had been sitting with a book propped up against her knees.

She watched as Kyle's figure followed the door as it swung open. When he saw her, he paused for a brief instant, as if either surprised or having just remembered something. But all he said was "Hi," and then he moved across the room, where he sat down on the only chair and began to remove his boots.

Gillian managed a return, "Hi," but couldn't bring herself to move.

He barely paid her attention. One boot was tugged off and fell to the floor with a thud. He began on the second. His attention was directed exclusively to the heel of his foot. She might not have even been in the room.

"I can't stand this," Gillian said finally. She rose suddenly, flinging the book upon the bed.

She walked to the dresser, picked up her brush, held it, then put it down; she then turned around, faced him, waiting for him to say something. She stalked into the bathroom, closed the door, ran some water into the sink, splashed her face as the adrenaline surged, dried her face, opened the door, and found that he was standing near the bed, just looking at her.

"Why won't you speak to me?" she asked.

"Because you're asking me things that haven't an answer."

"You can't tell me what's wrong?"

"There's nothing wrong between us," Kyle said. "There isn't."

In a way that was something. For a second, at least, it was something. But in the next second it wasn't, because they were still not together. And she needed that—needed the closeness that they had shared before.

"Then why won't you tell me what's wrong? There's something wrong. You don't make love to me—"

"It's not you...."

She thought she was going mad. "Kyle," she said, knowing that she was sounding like a crazy person, "everything's wrong, changed, weird, incomprehensible. And it hurts!" Her voice had a pleading, desperate, even shrewish quality that she had never suspected was a part of her personality. "Is it...is it someone else?"

From his blank expression she saw he didn't understand.

"Some other woman? Did someone come back into your life? Or maybe someone here...I—"

"No!" He shook his head, and if he hadn't looked so sad, he would have seemed almost amused by the idea. "No other woman. Of course no other woman."

"Then—"

"Look, I just need to work something out for myself... by myself. It is something only I can do."

"I want to help."

"Then leave me in peace, Gillian."

And his voice was so cold that she had no other opening to touch him with her love. She merely nodded.

That night he held her close to himself, but made no move to touch her beyond that.

Into the dark she whispered, "How long, Kyle? How long must I leave you in peace?"

But he didn't answer. She could only hope it was because he was asleep.

Chapter Eleven

It was high noon. Gillian glanced at the burning sun, seeing it the way millions of moviegoers would one day view it in theaters across the world. She already knew the scene well. She had viewed it on Kyle's storyboard, where each and every shot had been thought out beforehand, nothing left to chance, every angle and cent that it cost accounted for. Within minutes a camera would record this same vision exactly as Kyle had planned, and she knew the singular shot was important to the mood of *Due West*. Kyle's dream was being spun in celluloid. Each picture, and there were thousands of them, was like an individual thread in a magnificent tapestry being woven slowly but certainly by a master artist.

Gillian shifted her attention from sky to land, where an artificial tableau was being carefully constructed to mirror a reality that had once existed, a time that was heroic, when people survived by their wits and their guts, when life was innocent.

The activity level round her suddenly increased. Filming was ready to begin. People took their stations. Kyle stood behind the chief cameraman, ready to direct the next sequence.

The location for today was Weed Junction's main drag, more accurately, its *only* street. Certain alterations had been made to buildings already standing— names were changed on signs, historical artifacts added to create a sense of the late nineteenth century—but otherwise Weed Junction's naturally decrepit appearance lent itself perfectly to the script. A few other buildings had been constructed on site, but these were only false-fronted affairs, propped from behind by scaffolding.

All eyes, including Gillian's, gravitated to Kyle. He had raised one arm, signaling for silence on the set. Everything, everyone waited. Then he nodded, and a man came before the camera with a small board composed of two parts. He raised one part and clacked it down, marking the scene and take for the cameraman to record.

The film began to roll.

Gillian watched as if from a darkened theater.

In the distance a giant dust devil appeared, tainting the air.

Oh—not a dust devil.

It turned out to be six men on horses. They were coming this way, thundering into view, riding right into the center of town.

These were desperadoes. Anyone could see that. Dark horses, dark hats, dark beards, dark squinty eyes were filling the camera's lens with the certain signs of evil.

All of this was the way Kyle had planned it, and it was working. Abhorrence would grip the audience, just as Gillian felt it overpower her in that moment as she watched from the perimeter.

They were shooting, shooting at the adobe buildings. Windows were shattering. Now they were shooting at the sun overhead, then firing at a lizard scurrying across their treacherous path. The lizard ran like crazy across the road.

A camera on a dolly swiveled to follow the reptile's desperate progress. The lizard was safe.

A couple of the men laughed wickedly, enjoying the worry they'd caused the poor creature. One man lighted up a huge cigar; another spit out a disgusting wad of chewing tobacco. These men were bad hombres, all right. They had mean, leering faces to prove it.

Gillian felt hatred. Audiences would, too. Wonderful, Kyle, wonderful....

The action continued.

The bad guys were riding again, laughing and shooting, and one of the men was swigging down some liquor from a flask.... All of a sudden a man stepped into the street. He was followed by two women.

Gillian caught her breath, her eyes widening in disbelief. *What?* She took a step forward, then stayed the impulse to enter the scene, knowing she would only make things worse.

The six desperadoes pulled back on their reins; otherwise they were clearly going to flatten the man and the women who had moved into their path. The faces of the horsemen registered surprised confusion. Gillian saw them look to Kyle for instruction, but there was no time to understand what he wanted them to do. They could only react to save their own skins.

Chaos reigned.

It was happening too fast for Gillian to piece together all the disjointed events. What she did understand was that this unscheduled disruption was strange and wrong and dangerous for all concerned.

For one thing, the riders were not expert horsemen. Two of them were barely managing to stay in their saddles. The horses had reared, forelegs flailing the air while they careened wildly about on their hind legs.

Gillian watched one actor fall and be swallowed up by a cloud of dust.

The remaining three desperadoes were being spun around, their horses out of control. They didn't look mean and tough anymore, but simply terrified and confused. The air was filled with moans and colorful expletives.

"Cut! Dammit! Dammit, John...dammit! What the hell is this?" Kyle's furious words cut through the pandemonium.

John Proudfeather, who had shed his jeans and cotton shirt for buckskin pants and a shirt decorated with beading that didn't look at all as though it came from Taiwan, said simply, "I warned you."

Kyle had moved into the center of the street. He faced John squarely, staring him down. "John, what you've done...you've no damn right—"

"I'm doing it anyway," said John. Slightly behind him, Pablita and Maria stood motionless in John's long shadow, their faces determined and grave. They, too, had abandoned their modern garb for feathers, paint and long, colorful skirts, the official ceremonial dress donned by women in some of the nearby pueblos. In spite of the fact that they had caused all this trouble, Gillian thought they looked terrific.

"I thought we were friends," Kyle said.

"Nothing personal meant," John returned evenly. "I've got something to do, you've got something to do. Only one of us can do what we want. And that person's going to be me." John looked about him. It was very quiet on the set, eerily still. Even the men who had fallen were motionless, watching the old Indians and America's number one box office movie star face off against each other in the middle of a Western town at high noon. The only sounds came from the horses, who were clearly still unnerved by the incident.

"I guess," said John, slowly measuring the scene in his mind, "this interruption has cost you a lot of money." He looked meaningfully back to Kyle.

"Yeah, try around the neighborhood of $25,000. And it's money I don't have to waste."

"I don't have a lot of time to waste, either. Look at me. I'm an old guy. Today I wanted to go fish. Instead I had to come here."

"No. You didn't. You didn't have to come here at all."

John raised his brows. "No? If I don't, then tomorrow there won't be any fish left for me to catch. There'll be cans floating around and cigarette butts.

And those paper diapers people leave out by the highway. Wouldn't be any room for the fish with all that junk floating around. So I had to take the time to come here today. Some things you don't want to do, but you got to do them anyway. Just the way life is.''

Gillian had slowly moved forward. Her eyes shifted anxiously from Kyle to John, while her ears strained to catch what was being said. Obviously there was a history to this conversation between the two men. The only thing she knew for certain was that both men were serious. This was not some idle prank that John Proudfeather was engaged in, nor did Kyle take it as such.

''I told you last night—''

''And I told you,'' John said, his voice never rising above a moderate conversational tone.

''You know I can have you kept off the set.''

''You could try. Probably wouldn't make it, though. It's hard to keep me out when I want in,'' said John with a laugh. ''I can be a real pest. Lot of folks have said that over the years. Guess it's true.''

''This is serious, John. What you've done here today has real consequences. Don't make me have to do things I don't want. There are laws that—''

''Your laws? Your laws are nothing. So just make sure you don't cause me to do things I don't want to do.'' Then he turned and started off, going down the middle of the street with the two women at his side.

Everyone remained silent, watching them. Then Kyle called, ''Okay, let's break.'' He checked his watch. ''Thirty minutes.''

The silence was shattered and people began moving about, talking among themselves about the unexpected drama they had witnessed, others taking up discussions related to their own personal melodramas.

Gillian hung back, wanting to go to Kyle, but realizing that he needed to appear in control before the others. It wouldn't do to rush into the picture right away and make more out of the situation than what had already occurred. Gossip on the set abounded anyway, and a sign of something going wrong could affect the picture negatively. She didn't want Kyle to lose face. He was a hero in everyone's eyes—including her own. Heroes looked best when they stood alone, triumphing over insurmountable odds. At the moment Kyle was being cool, or trying to give that impression.

He had made himself busy, shrugging off the unpleasantness as if it had never happened. No one watching him would suspect he was concerned over the incident with John Proudfeather—no one but Gillian.

The telltale signs were subtle but evident—the way he ran his hand through his hair and took out a handkerchief for no reason, then put it back into his pocket, opened a clipboard, but stared above it, and finally, with it still in his hands, looked beyond to where John Proudfeather and the two women continued to march slowly, regally out of town.

Off to one side, standing beneath the porch roof of the Kachina Kantina, some members of the technical crew—a woman and three men—were hooting it up. Two of the men started to mimic an Indian war dance. The woman made a derisive remark about John

Proudfeather. Didn't the old coot know that the Indians had already lost the war?

Kyle whirled about, his gray eyes sparking anger. He took a step in her direction, then stopped, regaining control with obvious effort. But the laughter and dancing had died. The quartet stared at him, tense.

"The man believes in something. He just put himself on the line for what he feels is right," Kyle said stonily. "You have anything you believe in?"

No answer came.

"I didn't think so," said Kyle.

Gillian was on her way to join him, but he was quick to leave, turning immediately to stride to the hotel.

He was already in their room when she caught up with him.

He was staring at his face in the mirror when she entered. His eyes were red-rimmed, and for the first time she saw how tired and worried he was.

"Kyle?"

At her voice, he lowered his eyes from his reflection. Turning, he said almost angrily, "Okay... you want your questions answered? Why not? Let's get it over with. Now's as good a time as any."

Gillian sat quietly on the edge of the bed as Kyle paced, telling her in fits and starts about the man who had come to Weed Junction.

"The man in white..." Gillian said, thinking aloud as she pictured the past. "I saw him—he was looking around. He didn't seem ordinary, not like one of the usual tourists. I could feel that there was something wrong about him." She shook her head. "Funny, I always thought bad men wore black."

"Only in movies."

When Kyle had finished with all the details, including his conversation with John Proudfeather the night before, Gillian remained thoughtful, digesting the facts. "You can do something to stop them, can't you?"

"No. I either play along with them or I get out. It's what you call being between a rock and a hard place."

"But it's illegal—it's blackmail."

"It's life. At least one part of it."

"No," she said angrily. "No. There's got to be a way. If we can talk to these men, explain what you're trying to do, then they'll—"

"Gillian, my God, don't be so naive."

"All right, so they aren't Boy Scouts. But you haven't even tried to—"

"To do what? There aren't any names—there are no names and no faces to these men. Do you think they're so stupid that they would let themselves be known? Why do you think they hired this guy to come into town to deliver their message? Because they're smart and tough and they're not taking any chances on getting caught. This guy Baylor they sent here is a heavyweight—he's not some messenger boy sent around to deliver pizzas. And I don't know how to fight invisible men."

"We can find out who they are. We can expose them."

"Sure. But how?" Kyle said. "Gillian, I don't have time to run around peeking in keyholes. I'm on a budget that's so tight if I drop a dime in the dirt I'd have to bend down and pick it up."

"But you don't have any other alternative. You've got to stop them. If you don't, if you just pack up and walk out of here, you're going to lose everything you've put into the film.''

Kyle didn't say anything. The silence continued, and still he didn't say anything.

Gillian began to understand. Of course he hadn't wanted her to know about the demands being made on him to fund the development of the property around Weed Junction. His concern, however, wasn't that she be spared the worry of seeing him lose the shirt off his back. It was because he was going to keep that shirt on—that was why he had avoided answering her questions.

It was unbelievable. It was simply preposterous that the man who had shared her ideals, not to mention her body and soul, could now betray their mutual beliefs.

No, she thought, seizing upon a desperate hope, this couldn't be. She had only misunderstood. There was some missing piece of information she had overlooked. Kyle would explain what he really meant to do.

"Kyle? I know you don't really intend..." She gave the lightest of laughs, searching for the joke that was going to materialize when they both saw how she had misread his intentions. "I mean, you aren't going to go along with—"

The gray eyes were pools of misery. "Gillian, I don't have any choice."

Gillian laughed, then looked away. Her heart was rushing to flee her thoughts. "I don't believe it...."

"Gillian—"

"No!" She silenced him. "No, no...." She shook her head as a dog shakes itself after a swim, ridding itself of an unwanted condition. "It's not true."

Kyle came to her, put his hands on her shoulders. His touch was tender, meant to console, but she jerked herself up from the bed, unwilling to be touched. Such care, such love seemed a mockery now.

"Please...Gillian." His arms had fallen to his sides, the broad shoulders seeming to slope in dejection—a portrait of the hero in defeat. "Try to understand my situation."

"I understand," she said coldly. "Perfectly."

"Then you know I don't have a choice."

"You have a choice." The sentence was uttered over a muffled sob. She bit down on her bottom lip, fighting the impulse to fling herself into his arms and scream at him to come back to her, her Kyle, the man she had known and loved, who had suddenly been replaced by this stranger she didn't recognize. "Scott had a choice, too. Even I have a choice." Her suitcase was in the corner. Barely able to see through her tears, she grabbed it blindly and threw it onto the bed.

"What are you doing?"

"What does it look like I'm doing? I'm making a choice. That's what I'm doing." She flicked open the metal locks. "I'm not going to stick around here and see what's going to happen because of your choice. I thought you were someone you aren't. I don't seem to be very smart. But then, you said it, didn't you? I'm naive. I believe all the wrong people—"

"No!" Kyle slammed the suitcase shut.

Gillian hung her head, staring down at the bed.

Taking her by the shoulders again, Kyle forced her to face him. "I love you. I *love* you. I didn't lie to you—everything I said, I meant."

"Then put your money where your mouth is!" Gillian said angrily, breaking free of his hold. "Your money, your precious money, Kyle!"

"Gillian," he said, his voice edged with desperation, "why can't you see? If I make *Due West*—"

"I only see that a lot of people are going to make a mess of this area."

"But a lot more people are going to see my film. And those people will . . . oh, I know it sounds pompous, grandiose, but they'll have their consciousness raised. Kids will grow up and become adults, and they can protect other land."

"But you *are* able to protect it. Now. All you have to do is get out of here. If you don't even care enough to defend your own ideals, why do you think others will? Leave here, Kyle. Money comes and goes. But the land doesn't. There's only so much of it, and when it's gone, then what?"

"Gillian, I love you!"

"And I love you!"

"Then stick by me."

"I can't, Kyle. Because if I stick by you, I'm not sticking by me." He went to hold her again, drawing her to himself, but with a violent shove and a cry of forlorn misery, she pushed herself away and ran from the room.

She raced through the hall, down the stairs, the clatter of her footsteps mingling with the clamor in her mind. She was possessed by craziness, buffeted into a frenzy of action by fury and self-righteousness and fear and sorrow.

Downstairs she stopped, almost with surprise finding herself in the lobby. Carrie was sitting on the sofa, reading. Stella would be at the Kachina, or else she was out playing minor movie star with some of the real actors from Hollywood. Stella liked to run lines with them; she never got tired of being someone else. How Gillian wished she had that talent. About now, she'd trade herself in for anyone else's life.

Carrie looked up, idly taking in Gillian's presence.

"What's eating you?" Carrie asked, staring over the top of her magazine, a gossip rag whose banner headline claimed that a man in Iowa had discovered statues from the lost island of Atlantis in his cow pasture.

"Same thing that's got you," Gillian returned edgily.

Carrie looked more interested. She lowered the magazine a little so that her nose showed along with her pale eyes. Her nose was a touch pink, as if she had been crying recently. "A man?"

"I don't know. Maybe a man. Maybe just life in general."

"I hate men. I hate life. I hate everything." Carrie paused, but rather than launch into a more extensive account of her own miserable situation, she said selflessly, "Wow, like really...you look totally out of it."

"I'd like to be out of it."

"Go have a drink," Carrie said. "That'll do it. Always helps Stella when she gets weird. Myself, I don't need chemical crutches. I read about other people. Lots of them are much worse off—real disasters. Cheers me up."

"I don't drink," Gillian said, wondering why life, even when it was black, seemed so much easier to handle for other people. Carrie read, Stella drank, and all she could do was hurt.

"Learn." Carrie's face disappeared again behind the bold headlines.

So why not? Gillian thought, staring at the back of the newspaper. To drink away her problems was reckless and completely out of character, but she didn't care. Her sterling live-by-the-rules-personality hadn't done her a whole heap of good so far. What she needed was a few steps in the wrong direction.

She took them.

Gillian pushed through the double swinging doors of the Kachina Kantina and entered another world.

Nobody seemed to notice that she wasn't by nature one of them. In fact, no one in the saloon paid much attention to her, period. Oh, there were a few idle glances from men at tables, glances that followed her as she made her way through the smoke-clouded room. Otherwise people were tied to their own conversations.

At the bar she ordered a tequila.

"Make it a shot," she said. The bartender gave her a peculiar look, but she got her order a moment later, along with a saltshaker and a wedge of lemon. She had seen others do it, so like a professional she made a fist with one hand and poured salt between thumb and index finger. Then she squeezed a bit of lemon into her mouth, took a lick of the salt, and in one gulp downed a swig of the potent, colorless liquor. The tequila traveled like a hot snake down her throat. She could feel it in her chest, powerful stuff, serious alcohol. She was very pleased with herself.

"Another, please," Gillian said, and was immediately sorry she had added the polite word. She wanted to be hard and in control.

The second tequila went down. More suffering. But it was starting to be worth it; there was a tingling in her nose, a certain sign that her consciousness was on the way to being altered.

After that there was a third shot, and at that point she knew that she had definitely passed her limit at two. But it was too late. And Stella Sanchez was there to tell her so.

"What the hell are you doing?" Stella demanded, sidling up to where Gillian leaned against the bar. With an expression of marked disapproval, Stella eyed the three empty shot glasses. Gillian had insisted the bartender leave them there. They were hard-won trophies, signs that she was fighting back at life.

"I'm drinking tequila shots. As you can very well see."

"You? Ha!" Stella laughed scornfully.

"Why not me?"

"You don't drink. That's one reason."

"So what's this? You call this chopped liver?" Gillian swept an unsteady hand over the small, empty glasses.

"I call it stupid is what I call it."

"You know, Stella, you are always right." Gillian looked at Stella, who was not in clear focus. "You are the wisest woman I have ever known." She said it truthfully and with a feeling of wonderful, unbridled hostility.

"My supreme intelligence is a fact that goes without saying. Like the stars above, my common sense and good judgment are facts of the universe. All the more reason to listen up. Now, however, I'd like to hear from you." Stella paused, raised one eyebrow, and leaning against the bar, said, "So? Tell me. Out with it. What's this all about?"

Gillian turned her eyes back to the bar. "I'm leaving."

"Yeah? So what else is new?"

"In more ways than one, Stella. Gillian McGuire is taking off. And this is my goodbye party. I'm the only one who showed up, though. Until you, of course."

Stella nodded, appearing thoughtful. "You're serious."

"I am."

"Why are you leaving?"

"Time to go. When you gotta go, you gotta go."

"Maybe you need a new watch."

"Look, Stella..." Gillian turned again. She wasn't feeling very well. Things were starting to waver. Maybe, she thought, she had done it wrong with the tequila. She was, after all, no more than a rank amateur at this business of lightening her load of misery. Maybe that was why the bartender was constantly eyeing her so strangely; he recognized the ineptitude and knew where the folly would lead. But Stella was waiting and Gillian marshaled her faculties to present her case. "The thing is, sometimes a person has to know when to go. I came, and now it is definitely time to head out of here. You see, putting it in more epic terms—since we are, after all, here to make an epic— when a lone man rides into a western town on his lone horse and does something brave, he then gets back up on his horse and leaves the town. Because if he didn't, if he just hung around, he'd become just another guy hanging around. In fact, he'd become a pest if he stayed. So I'm leaving," Gillian finished smugly.

Stella looked impressed. But then she said, "You're full of it, you know?" And Gillian realized she had misjudged Stella's response.

Stella pointed the nail with the teddy bear on it, saying to Gillian, "You, number one, are not a mysterious lone stranger on horseback. You're a city woman with an old beat-up car—a city woman, may I add, who can't hold her liquor. Number two, even if you were some romantic-type figure coming in off the high plains, you haven't done anything here that even remotely figures to be a heroic deed. No way are your taillights going to be trailed by a cloud of glory. So basically, what I'm saying here is—you don't qualify."

"I am speaking in metaphoric terms. A person who stands up for their own ideals...there's a heroic gesture in that."

"Metaphor—what? This is a weather term? All I know is this tequila and strange talk is about a man. Your aura's cracked—a sure sign of a broken heart, clear as day to someone who can see such things— which I, of course, can. I'll bet you've had some sort of lovers' spat with Mr. Movie Star. Am I right?"

Gillian took time before answering to note that for once Stella was dressed normally. Instead of looking like an Albanian folk dancer, she was wearing a nice plain skirt and sweater. It was somewhat disappointing.

"No, you are not right," Gillian responded, getting back to Stella's insults and accusations. "For once, Stella—just this once, you are not right. This is not a lovers' spat, as you so trivially put it. There are far more serious issues at stake then petty quarrels concerning male and female egos.''

''I love it when you do that college talk. It just goes to prove you don't learn anything. You learn nothing about life that'll do you the least bit of good. If I'm glad for one thing, just one thing, it's that I had the good sense never to sink so low as waste my mind like that.''

''Knowledge is its own pleasure, its own reward. It doesn't have to have a practical payoff.''

''Well, that's good. Because in your case, it certainly hasn't paid. Still, I'm open. I'm able to absorb other viewpoints, so try me.''

''There's no point—''

Stella waved a hand. ''Please...educate me. I'm waiting. What are the big deal issues?''

''There's nothing to discuss. Everything's finished.''

''Yeah? Well, if it was all that finished, then why are you standing at the bar getting snookered?''

''Goodbye drinks, as I said.''

''I see.'' Stella paused. She sighed and shook her head in mock despair. ''So, tell me, what's that tear doing on your cheek?''

Gillian couldn't feel her cheek. Her cheeks had gone numb along with her nose. But her finger could feel, and with it she located the telltale moisture. She was a little surprised, not to mention embarrassed at being found out.

''So I was right again. As always.'' Stella grinned smugly. ''Petty egos. Male and female stuff. And you're running away again. From yourself. Typical.''

Stella nodded, then moved off, as if Gillian wasn't worth any more of her time.

The bartender caught her eye then, nodding to the little shot glasses. Did she want another hit? No. She was going back across the street to pack. Tomorrow she would set off.

She paid and left, walking unsteadily past others who were having, from the sound of it, a very good time. The tequila made her lighter so that rather than walking, she floated. Her head did not seem quite attached to her shoulders, but the space between the two did not matter. Nothing mattered. She wondered why life could not always be so easy.

But when she passed Stella, who was talking to the script supervisor and a production assistant, she felt the other woman's eyes latch onto her back and ride with her all the way to the double doors. That seemed real enough. The weight of Stella's dark stare rested heavily on her, and Gillian was glad when she pushed apart the swinging doors and slipped through to freedom.

Outside, the contrasting brightness was enervating after the hazy interior of the Kachina Kantina. Nothing much was going on outside. What had been the recent site of a showdown between white and red man was now a peaceful setting, where the only excitement was the galloping romp of two horses, corralled behind a redwood fence off to one side. A couple of security guards patrolled lazily from opposite ends of the street.

Gillian was halfway across, on her way back to the hotel to pack before her self-confidence waned, when Stella called from behind.

"Hey, you! You there—college girl! I've got something to say to you."

Gillian turned, still backing toward the hotel as she responded. "Later, Stella. I've got things to do."

But Stella wasn't about to give in so easily. "What do you have to do?"

"I'm packing." Gillian was still backing away. Stella was still coming forward.

Their voices weren't loud, but in the empty street their words seemed to carry far beyond the normal conversational range. If she didn't want to have everyone in Weed Junction know her business, Gillian could see that she was going to have to stop and deal with Stella.

"Packing. Running away. Typical, typical, typical." With the last "typical" Stella came to a stop. She was a foot from Gillian. Her arms were folded across her chest.

"Look," said Gillian, "will you just not start. This is *my* life. I'm entitled to live it in *my* own way. Right or wrong."

"And you're *my* friend."

"Fine. I'm your friend, you're my friend. Then let's just keep it that way. Back off, Stella. I know what I'm doing."

"Okay, so what are you doing?"

"I'm standing up for something that I believe in."

"Yeah?"

"Yeah."

"That's what you're doing, huh?"

"Exactly."

"No, you aren't. You're running away. Again. You're running away just like you always run away, because you don't have any guts. You take the easy way out, and then you mope around feeling like you lost some big battle or something, and you feel sorry for yourself for another hundred years. But you never went in there to fight to begin with."

Gillian felt the color drain from her face. "That's not true."

"Isn't it?"

"I made my statement at the city hall that time."

"So what? You should have come back again. You should have screamed all your complaints at the newspapers. You went in without enough ammunition, is all. You should have gone home and reloaded, turned around and come back blasting. And as far as your husband goes—well, that sorry excuse of a man wasn't worth the trouble. Of course, we know that now, but at the time you didn't know what a jerk he was. And you could have fought for him, too. Instead, you just wimped it out of his life. Now something's going on with you and Kyle, and even though I don't know what it is, I know like I know my own face that that man is crazy in love with you." Stella took a deep breath. Her eyes were very bright, and Gillian suspected Stella's face was as flushed as her own was pallid. "Let's put it this way—whatever it is, you stay put and see it through. If you leave now, if you just run out like this, then I don't want a letter from you later. You're not my type of person."

Stella didn't stick around for the answer to her ultimatum. With one last look at Gillian, she turned and marched off to the Kachina again. A moment later, as Gillian stepped into the lobby of the Weed Junction Hotel, she heard the Kachina's jukebox start up with a Linda Ronstadt song. The volume was particularly loud.

The break was over, and just as she was on her way up the stairs, Kyle passed her coming down. Seeing him, her heart gave a little kick. It reminded her of the way it had been when they had first met, both of them going in different directions. And it was still the same.

His eyes searched hers for hope, but she averted her gaze and moved past him. Anyway, there was nothing left for them to talk about now. Everything had been said, and only action could change the situation. They both knew that.

An hour later, after she had packed her things and put them temporarily into her old room—now being used as a storeroom for Kyle's personal effects and some of her own things, too—she got into her Mustang which was parked at the edge of town where it was out of camera range.

This time she didn't look back as she took the dirt road out of Weed Junction.

Chapter Twelve

Surprisingly to Kyle, the afternoon's shoot went without a hitch. But though this positive contrast to the morning's upheaval should have made him feel better, it had the opposite effect. Success was not a panacea for the aching, empty sense of loss he experienced each time he turned and found Gillian's face missing.

The happy days with Gillian were over. They had ended the day Dirk Baylor came to town. Kyle knew he had only been able to postpone the inevitable—that which had occurred three hours ago, when he had watched helplessly from behind a camera as Gillian left the hotel and walked to the outskirts of town, where cars and trucks had been parked while they filmed.

At the time she left, he had been locked in a heated debate with the cameraman, who said the angle Kyle wanted was impossible.

"Do it, Gene! Just do it, or get the hell out of here!" Kyle flared.

The man blanched, and for a moment Kyle himself was speechless. The outburst was totally out of character and certainly unwarranted. Kyle shook his head and said, "Gene, I'm sorry... forget that, please. It's not a good day. Shoot it however you think it'll work."

And when Kyle looked again, there was nothing to see of Gillian but the tail of the Mustang fading from sight down the road leading out of Weed Junction.

Somehow he was able to push through the rest of the afternoon. Inside he was shaky; outside, nothing seemed real. When filming had ended for the day, he couldn't bring himself to go back to the room he and Gillian had shared. Instead, he accepted the invitation to join the others at the Kachina Kantina. At least for a while he didn't have to be alone with himself and the truth that he had lost the biggest part of his life.

He was halfway into his second beer when the pain sliced through his gut. The scene he was part of blurred, and he clutched the bottle with both hands.

"Hey, you okay, buddy?"

The words came as if from the end of a long tunnel.

"You doin' all right there?"

The pain subsided, then was gone. All three men who had been standing with him showed embarrassed concern on their faces. No one liked a hero to falter.

"Chili," Kyle said, looking up from the bar top. He uncurled his fingers from the bottle. It took him a moment to focus his thoughts. "Killer stuff."

The faces relaxed. Talk began immediately about how many peppers this one had eaten on location in Veracruz; another told of *wasabi*, the green Japanese horseradish that could clear out sinuses for a month with one glob; and there was some minor bragging about consuming enough curry to send a rocket to the moon. Kyle couldn't help wondering if all this manic jocularity was for his benefit, or to lighten the scare for themselves.

Kyle listened long enough not to arouse suspicion, then excused himself, claiming he had a call to make from his hotel room.

He made it across the street and upstairs in time for the second wave of pain to sweep through his gut. Bursting through the door, he slammed it behind him and staggered to the dresser, where he held tight to its sides as he collapsed against its front, riding the savage, blinding pain to another finish.

Trembling, he jerked open the dresser's top drawer and pulled out the small leather kit holding routine first aid products. Beads of sweat coated his forehead and he rummaged around for the small plastic bottle with its remaining tablets. Thank God he had kept them even after the doctor had told him they wouldn't be necessary. Kyle had almost heaved them into the trash, along with the rest of the reminders of that bleak period of his life when he had waged his war against cancer. But the pills had been expensive, and he figured they might come in handy if he ever had a toothache in the middle of the night.

Only this was no toothache. And he hadn't had any chili for lunch, either. This was . . . this was like before with the cancer, the only difference being that the pains had begun more gradually then. To no avail he had doctored himself with antacid tablets and excluded spicy food from his diet, even eschewing coffee for herbal tea. Of course none of his measures had had any effect on the cancer. And then one day he'd found himself in a doctor's office, face-to-face with the truth.

He downed the pill with a glass of water from the bathroom and lay down on the bed. In five minutes the drug would take effect. After that the pain might come again, but he wouldn't feel it.

He wished there was something for the fear. Before meeting Gillian he'd felt he had made peace with the idea that he might not live forever, that perhaps he had only a year or two left of his life. There were no guarantees that the cancer wouldn't return. So he'd learned to accept his mortality. All he had wanted was to have the chance to film *Due West*. Then death could take him; there'd be no kicking or screaming.

But he had met Gillian and fallen in love, and everything had changed. Never had life seemed so sweet and full and vital. And the future—the future shimmered in his mind, golden and perfect.

Or it had until Dirk Baylor had left his calling card.

The pills could block out pain, and he could learn to live with the fear of cancer, he supposed. But what in hell was he to do about Gillian? How could he bear the loss of Gillian? This was the worst hurt.

He closed his eyes and there she was—laughing and beautiful, his Gillian. No, he thought, not *his* Gillian anymore.

The woman seated behind the large desk wore an expensively tailored gray suit and a string of white pearls. Gillian could not imagine the woman ever doing anything as plebeian as taking a shower or shopping for eggs and milk in a supermarket. The way she looked, she might have been the wife of the president of the United States, not merely a hired appendage to the governor.

In contrast, Gillian had on jeans, brown Western boots and a black sweatshirt, the sleeves bunched to the elbows. Even the weather was against her, her hair being particularly curly that day. It ranged bushy and wild about her face, and any attempt to comb it into place only produced a storm of static electricity. Pretty obviously, judging by the woman's discreet once-over, Weed Junction chic fell sorely short of the mark outside the city limits.

"I'm sorry, but he's away at the governors' conference," the woman replied to Gillian's request for an audience.

"He'll be back soon?"

"He won't be returning until Thursday."

Three days away, Gillian calculated with disappointment. She was a dope to come bursting into the capitol building without having first called to set up an appointment. That was clear enough now. Of course at the time she had left Weed Junction two hours before, it had seemed like a good enough idea.

"Perhaps someone else can help you?" the woman suggested with efficient curtness.

Gillian found her increasingly remarkable. Her lips barely moved. There was nothing mobile about her face at all, as if even a smile would be considered a forbidden excess of emotion.

"No. Thank you," Gillian replied, "but it's best that I speak to the governor himself." Then she added, because it would sound stronger, "It's important that I speak only with him."

"Yes, well, I hope you understand that the governor would of course like to accommodate all his visitors, but unfortunately his schedule if very full, and all meetings are made on a priority basis...."

"I understand," Gillian said, "and I wouldn't even consider barging in here and taking up his time—or anyone else's—if it wasn't really important. Urgent," she added.

"I see. But as I have no way of knowing the exact situation..." the woman demurred. "Most issues are handled by those on the governor's staff who deal specifically with—"

"I know. I know. But you see, this is highly confidential, a potentially dangerous, even explosive situation." The moment Gillian heard her own words, she knew she sounded like some kind of weird alarmist crackpot. "Look, I know I don't look very...impressive. I just kind of rushed out without thinking about fashion or anything. But I have credentials—not credentials in a legal sense, but I'm not some maniac off the street. My name's Gillian McGuire and I'm an anthropologist—a cultural anthropologist. I'm getting my Ph.D. from the University of

California... all I've got left is my thesis, actually. Anyway, I've been staying in Weed Junction for the past three months or so, and—''

"Where was that?"

"Weed Junction."

"I'm not familiar..."

"Well, it's small. It's about an hour or so out of Santa Fe—down the highway. Where you turn off, there's a coffee shop sign, and behind it there's a plaque about the Indian war of—" Gillian broke off. "Anyway, that's not important. But I've been there for the last few months, in Weed Junction, working on a—"

"Are you from New Mexico, Miss McGuire? A resident, that is?"

"No. No, I'm not. Technically I guess I'm from California."

"I see." The blue eyes became increasingly polite behind the professional mask, and infinitely more removed from emotional involvement.

Gillian knew the woman was never going to help her. The most she was going to get from this well-turned-out ice cube was a polite turndown, and by the way things were going, she might not even get the benefit of the politeness. It wasn't as though this was all new to Gillian; she had dealt with this type of woman often enough in Vista del Bravo.

"No," Gillian said, "you don't see, because I really can't discuss the matter with anyone, unless it is the governor himself. To do so could have serious repercussions."

"Yes, well I appreciate your, uh, caution. But I'm afraid that unless I know what this is about, I can't really be of any assistance."

"It has to do with something illegal."

"Perhaps if you consult with the police, then."

Her voice had become patronizing. She had categorized Gillian and her eyes dismissed her with the next sentence.

"We really don't handle such things here." And that appeared to be that. The sentence had the social effect of a door slamming in the face. Without a pause, she reached across the desk and pulled a stack of folders toward her.

Gillian seized her last chance. "Do you know of a man named Dirk Baylor?"

"No," the woman said sharply. She didn't bother to look up.

Still, all hadn't been lost. Gillian had watched the response carefully, not just listened. And now she had to wonder if it had only been her imagination that the woman's hand had faltered as she leafed through the stack of folders.

For a brief, horrible instant, Gillian felt like knocking all the papers off the woman's desk. These people of power, or those having at the very least the trappings of power, who did nothing, who cared for nothing, who served only their own interests, were as criminal in their way as Dirk Baylor and the men he represented.

Before she left, she noted the woman's name on the small wood and brass plate on her desk. Margaret Truit.

Rather than waste her time entirely, she spent the rest of the afternoon visiting one office after the next. Men whom Gillian hoped to see were either in meetings or out ill, or on vacation. Two men in The Department of Environmental Affairs were available to see her, however, and to these she confided her Dirk Baylor story.

They pretended shock, even made clucking noises signifying social conscience, but they also denied having the slightest knowledge of any such conspiracy as she suggested existed, and recommended that since she had no evidence, she might want to gather some to build support for her case.

"But I'm trying to get proof," she said. "That's why I'm here asking questions."

"Have you ever thought you might just ask someone you shouldn't?" the last man suggested. He, too, had light blue eyes, their color and quality resembling thin ice in Gillian's mind. "Could be dangerous," he said, and smiled.

Gillian dismissed herself, thanking him for his time, and feeling as she walked down the hall to the exit that she had just received a warning.

But of course there was no proof of anything she thought or felt. All she had done was to go from office to office, where she had been listened to politely by people who made her feel as though she was a delusional hysteric. She knew they'd have some real hoots when they talked about her later at the watercooler.

And could she really blame them? No, of course not. Her pleas were perceived as just so much air. No one could put a stop to what was going on, because as they said, there were no real names and no faces at which they could point an accusing finger. Dirk Baylor was someone they had never heard of in their lives. Gillian wished she had never heard of him either.

As she got into the Mustang, she glanced at windows that seemed to her like eyes all watching back, and suddenly she was very frightened. She realized with absolute certainty that she was in over her head.

And she knew that as much as she loved Kyle, she could no more put aside her deepest convictions than Kyle could bring himself to walk away from his film. It was hard, but she would compromise. He had asked her to stand by him, to understand his position, and she would do that. But along with her loyalty to him, she would be true to her own self, too.

As she veered onto the highway, she knew that life and love were one and inseparable.

Chapter Thirteen

Gillian wanted to drive straight to Weed Junction and rush into Kyle's arms. Every minute away from him was slow torture. How could she ever live through a total and complete break, if this pain of temporary separation was almost more than she could bear?

Still, as anxious as she was to rush back to Kyle and explain her absence and pledge herself to their future, it was necessary to make one last stop before seeing his face again.

As there was no proper driveway leading into John Proudfeather's small commune, she had to leave the Mustang at the side of the road and go by foot to the trailer and adobe house. They were easy to find; the friendly glow of lamps burning in both dwellings stood out against the gathering dark. From Maria's and Pablita's small house came the homey, comforting smell of burning logs.

But outside the night air was cold enough for a jacket, and by the time Gillian knocked on John's door, she was shivering. With her arms wrapped around her chest, she waited.

There was a sound from within, then a shadow appeared against the drawn window shade. A moment later John swung open the narrow aluminum door and, framed in light, stood before her.

He was surprisingly well dressed. He had on a natty red and black plaid woolen shirt, along with what Gillian recognized as a new headband. He also wore what looked to be new gray corduroy pants. Strangely, no matter what John wore, from clothes sometimes bordering on tatters in the summer to a surprisingly conservative outfit such as this current one, he always presented an air of contentment.

It struck her suddenly as she looked at him that she didn't know John anymore. Either he had changed, or else her understanding of him had been wrong from the beginning.

No longer did he resemble an old and simple Indian in decline. Rather than appearing diminished by his advancing age, he seemed to have gained in stature, as if the same light of wisdom that shone in his eyes also cloaked his frail bones, adding girth and suppleness to his form.

"Hi, John," Gillian greeted him uncertainly. "I was in the neighborhood. Thought I'd pop by, see what's happening."

He only nodded, seeming neither glad nor disturbed to find her on his doorstep.

"Mind if I come in?" she asked, looking beyond his shoulder to the trailer's interior as she hugged herself tightly against the chill air.

John had never invited her in before, and if she hadn't been cold, she probably wouldn't have had the courage to be so bold. Being pushy wasn't her style. But of course, a lot of what she was doing these days hadn't been her style until lately.

Her suggestion was considered; then, as if making a major concession to some principle, John stepped aside, allowing her to enter.

Inside, Gillian found John's living quarters surprisingly well organized and clean; most importantly the space was warm.

"So. You want coffee?" He started toward the kitchen before she could answer, more as if he wanted something to do than out of politeness.

"Yes...sure, thanks. Coffee would be great." Gillian kept her tone upbeat. What she had come here for wasn't going to put a smile onto his face.

She took a seat on the sofa. While John rummaged in his kitchen, opening cabinets and drawers, she was left to look about. She hadn't really known what to expect of John's style of living arrangement; if anything, she'd guessed he would have a typically chaotic bachelor pad, only maybe worse, since he was getting on in years and probably didn't care for order that much anymore.

Certainly she had never supposed John to be a reader, but her eyes fell upon a small bookshelf on which there were at least twenty to thirty books, mostly paperbacks, but also a few hard covers. Most were on nature, and there were some biographies of explorers. She even saw a couple of Castaneda's works on Indian mysticism among the other subjects.

"I didn't know you enjoyed reading," she called.

"You mean you didn't know I could read at all," John answered from the small galley kitchen that opened onto the formal living area. On the high counter separating the two rooms were various roots and dried plants in jars and bowls.

"I never really thought about it," Gillian countered diplomatically. It happened to be the truth. She had supposed that John had learned some English in school when he was young—enough English for him to get by in shops and tend to the administrative necessities of life. Apparently she had underestimated him.

John came around the counter and handed her a mug of coffee. The warmth felt good against her cold fingers, and she concentrated her attention on the rising steam, even as she felt John's eyes on her. She hadn't meant to offend him; that was the last thing she wanted. John could really make a mess of things for Kyle.

As if John had read her thoughts, he said, "I had to do that today. I didn't want to make trouble, but it couldn't be avoided."

Gillian nodded, looking up at him. "Yeah, well I kind of know what you mean."

John turned and went back into the kitchen to get coffee for himself, and Gillian's eyes strayed randomly to a small Formica end table wedged into a corner between the sofa on which she sat and a scaled-down armchair, its nubby tweed upholstery frayed in places right down to the filling. But what caught her attention was what was on the table, or more accurately, what was perched there. It was a stuffed owl, its condition every bit as disreputable as the chair's. The glass eyes glowed with bright intensity, reflecting the room's light.

"My good friend," said John, and Gillian looked up in surprise to find he had returned and was staring down at her with eyes as darkly luminous as the owl's. "Owls represent the spirits of people who have died. You can learn a lot from an owl."

He just stood there staring at her, and she felt as if he knew why she had come, and was only waiting for her to get to the point so that they could talk it out. The steam from his own cup rose before his brown face in waves resembling smoke. To Gillian he suddenly seemed far more than the old Indian man she had come to interview three months ago. A power radiated from the dark eyes, where mostly idle mischief had reigned in the past.

"I wanted to run away today," she blurted out, as if John had willed the admission from her. John merely gave one of his noncommittal nods. "But I didn't," she went on. "I couldn't. Couldn't. That's why I understand what you mean. Sometimes there isn't any choice to what you've got to do. It's funny, you know...." Gillian sighed, and when she took up the train of her thoughts again it was more of an internal dialogue than an explanation to another person. "It's like you can get away with a lot in your life when you don't really understand certain stuff. But once you understand, you're forced to do things you'd rather not do."

Breaking off, she saw that John was standing very still, listening.

What illumination there was in the trailer came from small directional lights built into the wall. The man's dark, deeply set eyes continued to watch her, glittering with either understanding or laughter; when his gaze took on that particular expression, Gillian could never tell if it signified ridicule or sympathy. Most often she suspected a combination of both.

"Anyway," Gillian said, coming to the purpose of her visit, "to be straightforward about it, what I came to ask is that you don't make any more trouble for Kyle."

She noticed tension in John's stance.

"Of course, I realize you've got a vested interest in your own campaign to save the land here. I appreciate that, truly, John. But I'm trying to deal with the same issue in a different way. I'm trying to do things legally, and I think that's the best way—for all of us. All I ask is that while I'm trying to settle things in Santa Fe, you don't cost Kyle any more expense, as you did today. And you're right, you've got a powerful weapon to use against him. You can disrupt everything on the set, and it'll cost him more money than he has. But Kyle's not the real enemy here. He's only a vehicle others are using to get what they want." When she paused, John's expression hadn't changed much, not enough to give her any hope that he'd go along with her suggestion. It was pretty clear he wasn't impressed with her speech; if anything, he seemed to have developed a slight smirk. An image from old cowboy flicks popped into her head: "White man speak with forked tongue...."

John waited, and when she didn't say anything else, he inquired, "That it?"

"Yes," Gillian said. "All of it."

"All of it?"

"The whole thing, yes. And I've been completely honest," she added, thinking that he might be remembering the bit about forked tongues himself.

He didn't say a word, and the silence between them deepened. When people didn't talk it made her nervous. A sense of panic rose in her—she couldn't let Kyle down.

"No!" Gillian said. "There's more. You're right—I've more to say. I love him. I love him so much, and I don't want him to be hurt. I'll do anything to keep that from happening—Kyle's a good man, a kind, decent man. He deserves better than this. If you go against him, John, then you go against me. And I'll fight you. I swear to you...."

Sometime during her tirade she had stood up, without even being aware of her action. Now she and John faced each other, she still trembling from the emotional storm, and John, as always, calmer, the dark eyes watchful, giving away little of whatever went on behind them.

Whatever response Gillian had expected from him, it wasn't what happened next.

John laughed. He began to laugh really hard, so hard that he had to turn around and lean his elbows on the small bar separating the living room from the kitchen. When he had finished, he looked over his shoulder and nodding at her, said, "That was good. That was real, real good. That was the best thing you've ever come up with." He thumped his hand against his heart. "That's where the power is. Okay, so maybe you have a chance. Maybe you can beat them, like you say."

As she left the trailer, John said, "One week. Then we'll end our truce. One week," he repeated, making it clear that she didn't have a permanent ally.

As she walked back to the car, it was so quiet that for a while she could faintly hear John laughing again in the trailer.

But on the way home to Kyle, Gillian cried as she had never cried in her life.

The tears came as a revelation. For the first time in her life, she knew what it was to totally experience love. It had flowed through her, complete and unobstructed while she had ranted on to John. She loved Kyle enough to forget herself; this love held power and strength enough to defeat a thousand men such as Dirk Baylor.

In a few minutes she would tell Kyle. Everything was going to work out for them.

Chapter Fourteen

How easy some of the most difficult things were to solve, even to conquer, Kyle thought, staring into the darkness of the hotel room; and how difficult it was to hold onto the most simple, accessible aspects of life.

For instance, the excruciating agony that had torn at his gut an hour before was completely gone now. It had been erased by a simple pill, and everything was okay—at least for a while. Merely by popping a capsule down one's gullet, it was possible to ignore a terrible unpleasantness like the possibility of one's death.

But there was no pill to help him forget Gillian.

Time, he thought philosophically, might eventually dull a bit of the hurt. But in the meantime he would have to endure the agony of each waking moment, aware that the only love he had ever known had ended.

Therefore he was left with reality. The cold, stark, merciless truth was simply that each of them had their own agenda to fulfill. He couldn't blame Gillian. He couldn't blame himself. All he could do was feel like hell.

And he could get on with what life he had left, for as long as he had it left.

The pains would return, of course, and he'd pop another and then another capsule into his mouth, but eventually the pills would run out. There would be no refill for the prescription until he went to visit a doctor. But not now, not yet would he allow himself to fall into the clutches of the medical profession. For one thing, he didn't have the time to squander on tests and on the exploratory surgery that would certainly be required; every minute he had left belonged to *Due West*. And anyway, there was no rush to confirm his worst suspicions by visiting a doctor, except to get the pills for the pain so that he could keep himself going through the process of shooting the film and the business of distribution. Being honest about his situation, he knew he could forget about waging another successful battle against the voracious mutant cells. Clearly they'd won the war.

When he was back in L.A. he would see his former doctor, the surgeon who was part of the cancer team that had worked the temporary miracle of prolonging his life. Realists though they were, they'd feel bad, of course, and he'd feel rotten, too—not so much because he was going to bite the dust, but because he was letting them down. Although they had been obligated to warn him that there were no guarantees that the disease wouldn't return, he had seen the glad excitement in their faces when they had presented him with a clean bill of health. They'd won one.

Listlessly Kyle reached for the lamp beside his bed and switched on the light. Then sitting up, he looked about the room, now barren of Gillian's personal effects. Absently he wondered where they had gone. He hadn't seen her carry away any suitcases or boxes that afternoon. But perhaps someone else had taken them earlier, before she had left.

A raw feeling of psychic pain, more acute than anything physical, ripped through him as he surveyed the places where her things had been only that morning, areas now vacant of any evidence that she had existed in his life.

Well, he'd have to fill up the corners of his existence as best he could. He wasn't going to have a lot of time to do it, either. But at least he would have the means. *Due West* was going to get filmed, even if he had to do it with one foot in the grave. Nothing else had worked out in his life, but he *would* have this.

Funny how life took its own turns. Fate, some called it. It sure had been fate when he'd met Blake Millman in the army, fate that Blake's father just happened to be a starmaker in Hollywood.

Blake Millman was pretty wild, which was why his family had shoved him into the army, hoping discipline would chill him out a bit. It was Blake who'd invited Kyle to Hollywood when they were both discharged at the same time. It had seemed like an innocent enough visit, but it had changed his life entirely.

For Kyle, entering Blake's world was like stepping from his seat in his hometown's lone movie theater, straight into the action on the screen. It was that incredible, that magical. There was the Millman house in Beverly Hills with its rolling green lawns and platoon of servants. There were catered parties beneath striped tents, and beautiful people to eat the exotic repasts that were presented on long banquet tables. There were laughter and music. Movie stars, producers, directors, writers and composers congregated at the Millmans', along with a whole assortment of other people who contributed their talents toward constructing fantasy worlds for a public disenchanted with reality.

The affection Kyle felt for them was sheer craziness, but they seemed to him like a family he had returned to after having been away for a long time. It felt like home, his true home. These people and others in their profession had made his life as a boy bearable. By proxy they had served as his mother and father, his brothers and sisters. Maybe it had all happened on a large silver screen, but they had given him lessons in friendship and love; they had instructed him on the merits of honesty and instilled into him the tenet that crime never pays.

He had planned on using his military educational benefits to study electronics, and was waiting to be accepted by the university when—just as in the movies he used to watch as a kid—life took a fateful twist.

Blake's father arranged for a small role for Kyle in a film a friend was directing. It was to be a way of making some extra money. That was the intention. Blake was also handed small parts now and then. It was an accepted part of the industry's nepotism—fathers hiring other fathers' kids. Generally the gratuitous opportunities never went anywhere, not unless one of the kids had a true calling.

Kyle was touched by Gordon Millman's generosity. Certainly Kyle could use the extra money to live on while he attended school. But he wasn't an actor by any stretch of the imagination, and he didn't want to let anyone down by flubbing the opportunity he'd been given. He couldn't risk jeopardizing the affection he felt flowing between his new friends and himself for the sake of just a few extra dollars in his pocket.

Kyle thanked Gordon Millman for the offer, but refused.

The refusal was not accepted. Blake's father liked playing God, Blake told Kyle with an ironic smile. He urged Kyle not to incur God's wrath.

So Kyle accepted the role.

He didn't care about the wrath so much, but he cared very much about the Millmans. Whether or not they felt the same way about him was immaterial. To Kyle, they were family. He would meet their expectations; he would be loyal.

Kyle had three lines. As far as he was concerned, they were the most important sentences that had ever been written in theatrical history. Those three lines had to be perfectly executed. He threw himself totally into his role, that of a doorman. He even began acting classes at a little theater to give himself confidence and to polish his delivery. The three lines were cut from the film.

There was some mix-up about his Florida high school transcripts. Consequently he couldn't make the next university admission date. He had to wait until the next semester to begin in electronics.

While he waited, he got another role through a casting agent who had seen him in a skit at the acting class. Blake's father was elated and took full credit for discovering and nurturing Kyle's talent. Everyone laughed, including Kyle.

This time he played a small-time hood in a gangster movie. He was killed off early, but his part remained intact.

It was the brightest moment of his life when he saw himself on the screen at the preview for investors, cast and crew at the Directors' Guild. Of course, the Millmans were there too. He liked the feeling of being part of something, of belonging to someone, of making people he loved happy. The little white bungalow in Florida was fading from his memory.

Electronics school was also forgotten.

Within six years, he went from bit parts to secondary roles. When he was twenty-seven he landed a screen role that brought him recognition by critics. He was touted as having potential for becoming a major talent.

A lot of things were said about him. Handsome. Rugged. An individualist. Kyle didn't know whom they could be talking about. He was always just himself, Kyle Dayton, the kid whose mother had said she'd be back, the kid who used to spend his life in dark theaters, pretending life was better than it was. No matter how many superlatives were hurled his way, he'd never outgrow that core of himself.

Still, on the outside he appeared to deny the past. He'd gotten taller, risen to six foot two in his stocking feet. Gone was the spindly frame of the eight-year-old boy; now he was broad of shoulder and narrow-hipped, had a body with solid legs and arms to warn men away and draw the admiring glances of women. The boy's tentative voice had grown deep and smoothly melodious, its inflections textured with all the past feelings he had never been able to share. His most exceptional physical feature, the trademark gray eyes with their golden flecks, were no longer haunted with yearning, yet they retained the mysterious element of a man who out of some dark necessity hid himself from others. It had taken years, but the overlooked child was gone; in his place, the adult Kyle intrigued and captivated, holding audiences in thrall.

The roles he played increased in scope and emotional depth; accordingly his earning power escalated steeply from what it had been starting out. And he was glad to be a part of a business that made him feel good. Movies kept little kids in hope and spun dreams for people who didn't have enough material in their barren lives to weave any of their own. In a curious way he felt that he was still going to the movies—just as he had when he was eight years old; only now he was on the other side of the screen.

Then one day he was presented with the opportunity to become a full-fledged screen idol. Without seeking or even wanting fame, it happened.

The offer came from Blake's father.

Gordon Millman had already been a major force in Hollywood when Kyle first met him. Now Millman was one of the top three producers in the industry. He wanted to catapult Kyle into the stratosphere. Kyle would star in a series of male adventure films that would make him a number one box office draw, and Gordon Millman would correspondingly become the richest producer in Hollywood. Certainly Millman saw himself as a living Hollywood legend.

That was the deal that was proposed. And Kyle's response was the same as before, when Gordon Millman had first offered him a bit part: Kyle demurred, afraid of failing.

Just as before, Kyle was worked around by Blake into saying yes to Gordon.

Everything happened as Gordon Millman had foretold it. Kyle became the year's number one male box office star; Gordon Millman was lionized as a legend in his own time.

Kyle should have been happy, but wasn't. Not that the films weren't entertaining—they were. But they had no heart. He, who had spent his childhood in theaters, could feel a movie's soul, and the ones that Gordon Millman was putting out were slick and characterless. Every time he left the rushes at the end of the day, Kyle felt hollow.

He had worked hard to perfect his acting craft, but what he was doing now had no meaning for him. The notion that life might actually *mean* something on a personal level came upon him with the force and surprise of a lightning bolt's direct hit.

He was thirty-seven years old at the time, thirty-seven years old by the time he woke up to the possibility that his life might have meaning.

Gordon Millman was more than surprised when Kyle turned down the contract to star in the fourth movie of the adventure series, he was furious.

Blake knew what he was talking about when he
warned Kyle about his father's wrath. On the subject
of vengeance, Millman demonstrated that he could
easily hand out lessons to God himself.

Kyle did his best to explain his position to the man
he had come to love like the father he had never had.
He had found a script, he told Millman. The script was
a good one—maybe even great. It was set in the
American West. This story had heart, Kyle said. He
wanted to do it.

Millman laughed.

He laughed so hard that he cried. When he had finished with his hysterics, he coldly told Kyle that he was
nuts. Westerns were as dead as silent films. Nobody,
including himself, would touch one with a ten-foot
pole—or more to the point, with even a ten-dollar bill
toward production costs.

Things got ugly after that. Millman called Kyle a lot
of names; ungrateful was the nicest among them.

The confrontation was shattering to Kyle. Still, as
he saw it, he was fighting for his life. There was no
choice in the matter.

Kyle believed in *Due West*. He read over the script
fifty times, and each time he saw it in his mind's eye
as a great movie, the kind of film that had carried him
through the bleakest days of his childhood. It meant
something to him; he was betting that it would mean
something to other people, maybe to some other
skinny kid whose life wasn't all that hot.

But he couldn't get funding. Even if he starred in it,
which had not been his original intention, there wasn't
anyone in Hollywood to bankroll his dream. There

were a few bites along the way, serious ones, but each time they fell off the hook.

Then it turned out that it was Gordon Millman who was cutting the line. Gordon Millman did not want to be crossed; he hadn't gotten to where he was by allowing other men to outmaneuver him. He had power in the industry, and he used it. The plan was to squeeze Kyle hard enough to make him come crawling back into Millman's own lucrative production.

That was when the stomach pains began the first time. They started gradually. Kyle took some antacid pills, tablets sold over the counter. Then his lower back started to hurt. He took aspirin for relief. It was tension, Kyle told himself. One day the tension forced him into the doctor's office. There were prods and questions, frowns and lab tests. The results came back. And then the diagnosis.

Kyle didn't believe it. Cancer was something that happened to other people. But he was lucky, the doctor said. Kyle had a fifty-percent chance of beating the beast.

There followed the operation and then chemotherapy and radiation treatments. He ate differently and thought differently, banished negative thoughts and visualized good cells felling the bad ones.

And it worked.

"Congratulations," said the doctor. Then he added his piece about nothing in life being for certain. Maybe Kyle had a long time to hang out on the planet; maybe not.

Life became exquisitely precious to Kyle after that. There was a sweet sadness to everything, because to him everything was so beautiful and so transitory.

There was an appreciation for even the smallest elements of life.

He wanted to make *Due West* more than ever. It was to be his gift to the boy he once was. It would be his gift to the other boys who sat today in dark theaters, wanting lives they didn't have. And it was for the man he had become.

He finally found a backer who would take a chance on his project: himself.

It took liquidating everything he owned to get enough cash to go into production. He cut as many corners as he could with cast and crew, and decided that he would direct and star. He couldn't even get delay insurance; although his medical problems had been kept out of reach of the press, the insurance company demanded an examination. Nobody was going to bet money on a man with odds saying that he could pop off at any time. So *Due West* wasn't merely being produced on a shoestring budget—no, like Kyle's life, it was dangling by a thread.

But all of that had passed, and now he had to move on, keep going.

Kyle rose from the bed and made his way into the bathroom, splashed cold water onto his face and dried it with a towel. There were things to do, and in spite of his unhappiness, he was going to have to push himself through each minute of every hour until he accomplished his goal. Gillian would have to be forgotten.

The first thing was to set up a new time and budgetary schedule, even tighter than the one he had already planned. Financially, John Proudfeather's stunt had cost him dearly.

For two hours he sat in the room, papers spread out on the bed and floor as he went over his plans. Every so often, absorbed in the technicalities of saving his production from collapse, the hurt would be blanked out. Then a break in his thoughts—and the pain would return. Gillian's face would appear before him, and he would find himself reliving the fleeting moments of joy they had shared.

Then, aching with loss, he would force himself back to his task.

For a record thirty-five minutes he had managed to avoid one of these troubling excursions into the past. His head was bent over a list of rented props that were to be delivered from a private resident in Taos—the owner being a collector of Western memorabilia— when a shadow darkened the paper he was studying.

A wave of cold fear passed over him. He turned his head, eyes raised.

"Hi," Gillian said softly, her voice wilted.

With concern, it struck him that she looked very tired, beaten down with fatigue. But then his mind raced again—Gillian had come back!

It was almost too much for him to accept. Slowly he rose from the floor, fighting against the impulse to pull her into his arms and rail at her for leaving him, for abandoning *them*. But of course he had no right to do that. There was no blame on either side. There was only the hurt, the devastation he had suffered in her absence. And now here she was.

He was elated.

Still, he could not trust his gladness. Five minutes ago he had believed he had lost her forever. Now cau-

tion made him hold back the hope that she had come
to stay.

"I didn't hear you come in...."

Standing before him, she seemed as uncertain in his
company as he felt in hers, an observation that provided him a small consolation.

"Sorry," she said, "didn't mean to creep up on you.
But I thought you were busy, so I didn't say anything.
Just watched for a while." For an instant her emo-
tion-filled glance seemed to strain to find something
in his.

He understood her longing for connection, and yet
he couldn't respond. It was as if he had lost the means,
just as she had, of communicating in a common lan-
guage.

Then defeated, or maybe just losing courage, she
dropped her attention to the papers strewn over the
floor and bed, and began again in a forced conversational tone. "I thought you heard me come in. So I
waited—I thought maybe you..." She looked back up
at him, her glance stricken. "That is...this afternoon we had a bad time here, so when you didn't say
anything, didn't turn around, well, I was afraid
that..."

Kyle ran his fingers through his hair. "No, no, I
didn't hear the door." He lowered his own eyes to
survey the sea of paperwork surrounding him. "I had
a lot to do—have a lot to do," he corrected himself.
"Budget stuff."

He looked back at her, and a little spark of joy ig-
nited in him at finding her still in his life. But no matter how much he loved her, he couldn't put himself
through the kind of pain he had endured this after-

noon. He couldn't just fall at her feet, grateful that she had returned—if, in fact, she *had* returned for more than a suitcase or a last look.

Gillian nodded. She raised her eyes again. In this lighting they were a deep forest green, shadowy as dense woodland. "John's little demonstration was expensive, I know. I understand what it cost you."

"And so did he," Kyle commented sardonically.

There the conversation floundered. Both waited, their eyes seeking from the other more than their words offered.

As a man, he had never considered himself remotely violent. However, suspended in the distance that lay between them, he suddenly found himself stirred by a primal urge. Domination.

It was a feeling totally foreign to him. And yet…he wanted to conquer her, to take her. In a purely and hideously uncivilized, masculine way, he wanted to force his will upon her.

Looking at her, available, vulnerable, feminine, beautiful, totally desirable in every way—he wished to own her. He wanted to possess her. He wanted to take her with his body and soul and mind, until they merged so completely that there would never be another chance of being separated from each other.

"John isn't exactly who I thought he was," Gillian said, and Kyle recognized a change in her eyes, but didn't want to analyze it; he wanted only to have her, wanted to stay with the honest simplicity of his desire to take her. The urgency was something to which he could totally respond, feel completely, and in it there was no room for question or the torment of doubt. "Maybe," Gillian went on, "maybe none of us is ex-

actly the same anymore...at least not who we thought
we were when we came here."

Kyle listened, but still only partially. The urge to
make love to her flowed hotly through his blood. With
the slightest movement of her head, her brown hair
shone in places where it picked up the light. Unkempt
and ruffled, the thick mane accentuated the smallness
of her face, casting her as a pretty doll, lovingly per-
fected in detail by some master artisan. He wanted to
hold her face between his hands, wanted to press his
lips onto hers, to feel once more the yearning need of
her body for his own and experience the eager invitation to enter into the rapture they knew so well.

But instead of acting out his male fantasies, he said,
"All I know for sure is John made a lot of work for
me."

"And for me. Today, I—"

"Gillian, look—you walked out of here today, and
I never thought I'd see you again." His words
brimmed with frustration. He was scolding, he was
passionate, he was desperately in love and desperately
afraid. "And now here you are, and we're talking
about papers and John Proudfeather." His voice had
risen, but he didn't care. "My heart's not a revolving
door. You can't think you can walk out and then walk
back into my—"

"But I haven't left! I didn't. That is, Kyle...I meant
to leave. For good. I have to be honest about that. I
wasn't just making a grandstand play about how I felt.
And I still feel that way. Except that I love you as
much as I love myself—and I love us together. So I
had to try. I couldn't leave without at least putting up
some kind of a fight."

"But you did leave," Kyle said coldly, the passion he had experienced a moment before dying in the light of fact.

"No, no... I went to Santa Fe. There was something I had to do there, and until I actually went through with it, I couldn't talk about it." There were tears coming down her cheeks, he could see. "I'm not brave, Kyle. I'm a coward, a worm, if you want to get right down to it. And what I did today was try to change that. I figured if I went to Santa Fe and found out who Dirk Baylor was—"

"You what? You did what?"

His tone caused her to flinch. Less certainly she continued, her voice almost too soft to hear. "I wanted to help."

"Gillian, what the hell are you telling me? What exactly did you do there?"

"Look, I went there to find out who he was—this Baylor guy—so that we could put an end to this blackmail operation they've got going. I was trying to trace—"

"Oh, God," Kyle moaned. He turned in a small circle, coming back to face her. "Gillian, tell me you didn't really involve yourself, you didn't actually go up to people and tell them what was going on here."

"I did. I involved myself," Gillian said half defiantly, half pleading to be understood. "Or at least I did my best to find out who Baylor was. Only I didn't. I failed."

"No kidding. Failed, huh? Wonder why?"

"Not because I didn't try. No one seemed particularly hospitable. Those who agreed to see me wouldn't give me any information that was helpful."

"You honestly thought someone would?" Kyle asked, incredulous.

"It wasn't a total impossibility. Anyway, I hoped someone might say something, that they might understand or sympathize."

"Then you're..." He held back what he was going to say, which was far more vitriolic, but certainly as accurate as what he did say. "...naive."

"Why not optimistic?" Gillian challenged him.

"Why not stupid?" he shot back, meaning to hurt her now, hoping to save himself through this anger he had mustered in place of the agony of needing and loving a woman he couldn't bear to lose.

With her eyes full and shining wet, she said in a voice that caught several times, words tripping on rising emotion. "I had to do it, Kyle. Can't you see, I had to do it for myself as much as for us?"

And then she stepped with a grace he found both heartbreakingly familiar and demonically irresistible between the papers and file folders scattered around the floor.

Her eyes never left his. No matter that he would suffer in hell for the rest of eternity for allowing her to enter his heart again, he was incapable of drawing away as she fell against him with a small cry.

Twining her arms around his neck, she half sobbed, half whispered, "I've lost myself, Kyle...lost myself completely. I love you so...how could I go? Where would I go? How could I leave my own self? That's what you have become—my very own self." She was close to him now, physically pressing the intensity of her love into him, as if words alone could not convey the feeling. "It makes me afraid, makes me helpless, loving you this way."

Fevered, half-crazy with his own fear and love and desire, he grabbed her tighter. "Don't go, don't ever leave me again." Over and over again he breathed, "Don't go, don't go..." as if the words could make it so, all the time knowing they couldn't.

They kissed, their need for each other ferocious.

Lifting her, he carried her over the papers, stepping on some, kicking others aside. It made no difference. The world was in his arms.

Placing her on the bed, he undressed her with feverish haste. She helped him, then ripped at his clothes, flinging each article aside.

Lying beside her, he stroked her hip, the velvet curve of her belly, explored lower, until at the pressure of his palm she shivered with small, barely controlled convulsions and guided him with her arms to lie over her. They were both ready, unable to wait another torturous moment of separation, and he slipped easily inside. Trembling, they held still, feeling the moment, experiencing the fullness of their love.

Kyle raised himself slightly to look into her eyes. He moved one hand softly against the planes of her face, brushing aside stray locks that had fallen across her lips.

"I love you," she said softly. A tear sparkled at the edge of one eye. "...love you."

"Oh, Gillian...love, love, yes. But do you trust me?" There was a hesitation, and immediately he felt a terrible sinking within.

There was no answer as she buried her face in his neck, pulled him down again, then kissed him with a fury close to being violent. "Make love to me," she urged. "Make love to me. I don't want to think. No questions. I only want to feel, to love."

Her breathing was shallow, coming in urgent gasps as he pressed his mouth against her collarbone, then moved to her breasts. Beneath him she began to move in a fluid, natural rhythm, carrying him along with her passion.

Whatever thoughts he had fragmented into an expanding bliss. There were no answers, no questions, no tomorrows, no yesterdays; only they existed, the steady tempo of their bodies spiraling onto level after level of pleasure, until, arching, Gillian cried out once sharply, then again on a longer note. Moving faster, Kyle, too, shuddered and stiffened, his head thrown back as with a low moan of ecstasy he joined himself with her.

The world had fallen away, but as the moon shifted slowly in the sky, reality was again illuminated. For two hours they had slept soundly, exhausted, cradled in each other's arms; now Gillian stirred beside him, and through sleep-laden eyes, Kyle watched as she moved across the room to the bathroom.

She was so beautiful, more beautiful than any woman had a right to be, he thought with an ache of wonder and love and with the glad fullness of contentment. And immediately, upon seeing her flawless body, his own responded.

"Gillian..." he said, and she turned, she smiled at the sound of his voice. Her eyes glowed in the light that came from the window, and he watched as her gaze fell, taking in his arousal. "I hope to hell you don't have a headache," he said, and she laughed softly, shaking a finger at him.

"Thirsty," she said, and ducked out of view into the bathroom.

Kyle waited, desire building with each second. He heard the water go on and the sound of the glass being filled. These little things took forever. He wanted her. She shut off the tap, and there was a space of silence. He heard the sound of the glass being placed back in the stainless steel holder over the sink, and then . . .

. . . a crash.

"Oh, damn . . . ! Sorry, it flew out of my fingers!"

Kyle froze. At the sound of the glass splintering, all desire, all happiness exploded. The future was a blackened mass of charred dreams condensed into one hateful word: *cancer.*

In his joy he had forgotten. How could he have forgotten? Only hours before he had drunk out of the same glass, swallowing a capsule that allowed him to pretend for a while longer that he could be part of life.

The breaking of the glass had jarred him back into the absolute reality that no amount of compromise or wishful thinking could take away; the fact that death waited for him.

Coming out of the bathroom, Gillian was talking to him. "I picked up the biggest pieces, but don't walk in there with your bare feet until the smaller ones can get swept away. I'll tell Stella first thing in the morning."

She was slipping into bed.

"Now," she said, snuggling against him, her hand coursing over his chest, then lower, lower. "Where were we?"

As gently as he could, he took one of her wrists into his hand and guided her fingers to his lips, kissing each one softly.

"Kyle?" She moved slightly, checking his expression.

"Sorry," he said, closing his eyes. "I guess I'm tired after all." And then, softly, added, "I love you."

Chapter Fifteen

Three days passed, during which everything seemed on the surface to be the same as before. Although they laughed together, ate together, worked together and made love together, it was *not* as it had been before.

What she and Kyle had before was perfect. Gillian wanted her romance back again. She wanted it back *exactly* the way it was. Now, instead of the free-flowing rightness, there was a self-consciousness to every moment they shared.

Once, while Kyle was shooting a scene and she watched from the sidelines, Gillian saw John Proud-feather move into position at the far side of the set, safely out of camera angle. He only watched, causing no trouble, but she saw Kyle tense as he, too, caught sight of the troublesome Indian.

Later that day at lunch, when she and Kyle sat together picking on portions of barbecued chicken, Gillian decided to be brave and said, "You don't have to worry about John."

Kyle stabbed his fork into the thigh, splattering thick sauce onto the paper tablecloth. "Sorry—worry's become my middle name lately."

He said it jokingly, yet beneath the brusque, careless remark Gillian recognized the deep truth of what he had thrown off as humor. Kyle had changed.

The signs were almost imperceptible, hard to pinpoint on a rational level, yet she could feel the difference. Although outwardly every bit as tender as he had been before their clash of ideologies, she sensed in him a kind of private withdrawal.

Twice she had come into their hotel room and felt his irritation at her unexpected presence. He had appeared almost jumpy, possibly even furtive. But the idea that he was hiding something from her was so preposterously out of character that she could even laugh away her suspicions by saying, "Hey... who'd you just stuff under the bed? A blonde or a redhead?" Still, she had actually been relieved when he had laughed. The laughter felt good; it was a part of the old times.

But the jokes between them were wearing thin, and his last effort at dissembling was just another failed attempt to avoid the issue. One of these days Dirk Baylor was going to come back.

With studied concentration, Gillian mounded what remained of her mashed potatoes, and speaking carefully, said, "John promised he wouldn't cause any more difficulty—at least not for a while."

"Really?" Kyle was about to take a bite. He paused, the fork held to his lips. "And how's that? Exactly." There was a sharp quality to his voice.

"Exactly? He promised me."

Kyle put down his fork and stared into his plate, as if reluctant to continue the conversation, but unable to withdraw.

"And I ask again, why is that?"

"Because," Gillian said, "I told him I needed a week to see if I could stop the plans to develop the area. I said I'd try to use legal means, the proper channels."

Kyle's gray eyes had darkened to a deep slate color, and his face had settled into a grim mask. "Why can't you understand? Gillian, these men are not to be bullied or coaxed into accepting some nice high moral standard that's meaningful to you. Life just isn't like that in the real world. It's not tidy and neat like in academia, where you follow rules and regulations and at the end of a semester you get a gold star or an *A* for your efforts. Dirk Baylor's dangerous, and he was picked to do his job by men who know that, men who are willing to go that far to protect their interests and further their own causes. If it were just a matter of making a few social calls and doing some glad-handing, don't you think I would do it myself?"

"Okay, okay," she conceded. "I get the point. But I'm willing to take a chance that maybe this is all just some big, dramatic bluff. Look, it's been three days. I'm still alive." Seeking escape from the unpleasantness, she looked off to where some members of the crew were filling their plates at the buffet table. "...and getting fatter by the day, eating those

brownies over there." With that she started to rise.
"Want to join me in a chocolate fix?" she asked,
looking down to where he sat. "Kyle? Kyle...!" His
face had gone chalk white, and his eyes were squeezed
closed as if he were suffering some excruciating pain.
"What is it!"

He seemed not to hear.

For an instant she stared, immobilized by panic.
Something was wrong... something terrible had happened. What had she said?

She opened her mouth, ready to call for help, but
just as she did, he reached out and took her hand,
gripping it too tightly, saying, "No... no... it's okay.
It's just—" He tensed, held his breath, then relaxing
slightly, said, "Something I ate—nothing major."

"Oh, oh..." Gillian laughed uneasily, relief flooding through her. "I almost thought..." She shook her
head, banishing the fatal vision. "Just something you
ate." And she laughed again.

A day later, the laughter was only a distant echo in
her memory.

"You paid him?" Gillian slumped, her back against
the door of their hotel room. It was three in the afternoon. They had stopped shooting early. Kyle stood by
the dresser, his head lowered, face in profile. "How
could you do it? You didn't even talk to me about it.
Couldn't you have at least—?"

"Talking about it again wouldn't have made any
difference in the outcome," Kyle intoned stoically.

"It would have made a difference to me."

"I had to do it," he said, turning his head so that
she could see into the gray eyes shot with their golden

sparks. "I'm not glad about it. I'm not proud of it. The way it was put, there wasn't any other decision open to me. So I gave them the first installment . . . to get things rolling on the road project, as Baylor phrased it."

Gillian leaned forward, moving away from the door. "Then maybe you could back out? It was just a first check, not the whole thing. In essence, no more than a stall." Gillian stalked about the room, fists clenching and unclenching as she thought aloud. "So there's still time to do something. We're not beaten yet. A little check, a measly amount compared to the whole enchilada they want, right? It's not over till the fat lady sings."

"What?"

Gillian looked at him, almost surprised to hear another voice. "Oh . . . you know, it's not over till it's over. When do you think the check will clear?"

Kyle shrugged. "Who knows? Baylor may have cashed it already."

"Good, good. . . ." Her mind was working. "The sooner the better."

"Gillian, no." His gray eyes bored into her. "*Don't.* Don't get involved."

"Why can't you understand? I keep telling you, I'm already involved. And you know what? Being involved feels good to me. It feels right."

Kyle was correct about the check. It had cleared almost immediately. Two days later Gillian had copies of it in her hand, endorsed by Baylor himself.

"I don't like what you're getting yourself into, Gillian," were Kyle's last words to her as she left for Santa Fe.

On the way there, she stopped long enough to shoot pictures with her camera of the road surveyors who were back staking out the wide route to be cut through the desert leading to Weed Junction. It took only an hour to get the prints developed when she reached the city.

In Santa Fe she presented her evidence—the check, the pictures—and told her story to an assistant to the Commissioner in The Department of Business, Transportation and Housing. Another man, from The Banking Department was called in to overhear her allegations. Again she was listened to considerately; copies were even made of her "evidence." Everything would be investigated; she had their word on that.

But words weren't good enough, Gillian countered vehemently. "What do you think? I'm naive? You think I don't know you're just humoring me—the madwoman of Weed Junction?"

The barely veiled smirks behind the polite replies told her the answer.

So she raised an enormous ruckus, demanding that her supposed allies gain audience with the governor—immediately and in her presence. It was quite a scene, one that she fervently wished Stella could have been there to witness, especially the part where the uniformed guard escorted her out of the state building.

Like some maddened general, she shouted, walking backward from the building, "I'll be back!"

Of course the guard didn't even bother to turn around, just disappeared inside the building, where he'd forget her along with the other occasional nuts who happened by.

She felt energized, even by her temporary failure. But upon returning to Weed Junction, Kyle saw her in far different terms.

"You don't have the power to do anything, Gillian. Making a scene may be good for your ego. It may help heal some old wounds. But it isn't going to get the job done. They'll just make you out to be a hysterical woman."

She didn't want to give him the satisfaction of knowing that they had already done just that. Instead she said, "Tell that to the people who marched on Selma."

"There were thousands."

"And Gandhi—"

"—was assassinated."

"Why are you being such a coward?"

For just an instant, it seemed her words had hurt. She started to be sorry. Attacking him wasn't fair. Then, calmly, he said, "It's all in the perspective. To you maybe I'm a coward. I call it being realistic. And along with that, I don't want to see you get hurt."

Two days later, her agreement with John Proud-feather not to cause any more trouble on the set expired. It was strange how once she had considered John nothing more than an ineffectual, crazy old Indian. Now he wielded enough power to put an end to Kyle's film and in so doing, stave off Dirk Baylor.

It was hard not to be angry with Kyle for not doing more; on the other hand, it was even harder to be angry with him. He looked dreadful. He hadn't shaved for the past three days, instead pushing himself out of bed after only four hours' sleep and putting on yesterday's clothes because apparently they were more

readily available than the clean ones stored in the
room's pine cupboard.

"Kyle," she said, watching him with concern from
her side of the bed that morning, "this schedule
you've set . . . it's not human."

"Maybe not. But it's necessary."

A moment later he left, closing the door on her.

Gillian was grappling with another change. Kyle
hadn't touched her for three days. He had made no
attempt to touch her affectionately in public or even
in private. Now and then she would make a physical
overture. She would pass him as he studied a scene, his
head bent to the page, and stop to rub his shoulders;
another time she would place a hand on his arm or
stroke his hand. Yet, instead of welcoming the attention, he seemed to shrink from her touch. She bore the
rejection by telling herself he was exhausted and
preoccupied. He also wasn't eating much.

"Do you want to talk?" she had asked, when he
came to bed at two o'clock the previous morning.
Kindly, the dark veiled her tear-stained face.

"I'm half-dead," he muttered. There was a pause,
and then, as if he had said something funny, he gave
a short laugh.

"I don't understand what's wrong. You're so
cold—"

"I'm tired, Gillian. Is that so hard to understand?
It happens sometimes. People get tired."

"But the film's going well. It's ahead of schedule
now."

He said nothing. He was asleep.

She touched him then while he slept, pretending
things were as before, when she could rest her face on

his chest and he would stroke her hair and tell her how much he loved her. But all she could hear was his breathing in the silence of the room.

By ten in the morning he had already been up for five hours, Gillian for three. She had waited for a call in the lobby of the hotel until that time—there being no private phones in the rooms.

Stella kidded her about being like a cat on a hot tin roof, pacing back and forth, watching the phone as if she expected it to escape. She knew what Stella wanted. Stella wanted to know what was so important about the telephone this morning. But of course she couldn't tell Stella she was waiting for a call from the governor, a call that she had been led to believe would come. One of her contacts had promised absolutely to tell him the complete story. Stella, like Kyle, would only have laughed and called her a dreamer.

John Proudfeather had taken to calling upon rocks and the sun, the wind and the clouds, not to mention pieces of twig and ordinary trees. And John Proudfeather seemed to be doing okay for a guy his age—a hell of a lot better than she and Kyle seemed to be doing. John Proudfeather, who came scouting around the set now and then, had never looked better.

At five after ten, Gillian gave up her impatient vigil and dialed the number of her contact in Santa Fe.

"Sorry," the man's secretary said, "he's not in."

"Oh. Did he leave any message for me?"

"No. Sorry, again."

"Well, is there anywhere I can call him?"

"Mr. Blickman's left for vacation and can't be reached. I'm—"

"—sorry. I know," said Gillian, and put the receiver down.

"Bad news?" asked Stella from behind the counter, where she was folding flyers advertising the Weed Junction Hotel that were to be passed out to relatives of the cast and crew when they returned to civilization.

"No news," Gillian mumbled, lost in thoughts of what to do next.

It was then that she saw him. Stella had left the door to the hotel open to the mild fall weather. Into the door's empty frame came two figures walking together.

Kyle was one of the men. His shoulders were high, held rigidly, arms tense at his sides, and not moving as usual with easy abandon in time with his long stride. Gillian almost didn't recognize his face. It was grim, bordering on haggard. The haunted look he wore did not belong to the golden movie idol she had met just a couple of months ago, did not belong to the man who had laughed and loved her so openly a month ago.

And next to him was Dirk Baylor dressed in a winter-white suit, his hands in his pockets. His own gait was open and relaxed as he spoke. He even kicked at a rock—just a Huck Finn at heart.

At the sight of her enemy walking with Kyle, Gillian's heart was pulled tight.

She moved into the open doorway, placing one arm against the frame for support. A sudden weakness assailed her.

The men had reached a black Lincoln parked on the other side of the road about twenty feet from the Kachina Kantina. The long automobile glistened radiantly, making a startling contrast to Baylor's white outfit.

Words were being exchanged between the two men. It was impossible to hear from where she was, but they had to be angry, impulsive words, for Kyle stepped forward menacingly as if to assault Baylor. Almost instantly, Baylor backed away, his right hand reaching into the upper left side of his jacket. Kyle froze, holding back, but his stance was still threatening.

Baylor didn't dawdle anymore. He moved closer to the driver's side, his hand wrenching open the door.

At the same moment Gillian moved out of the hotel, a surge of adrenaline carrying her over the hard-packed earth. There were no other people nearby, and her sudden appearance caught the attention of both men at the same time.

By their expressions, neither seemed glad to see her.

"You...Baylor! Just wait a minute!" she called, walking fast. He watched her with cold blue eyes. A year ago she would have withered beneath a stare like that; now it made her all the more determined. "I don't know who you are. Yet. But I'm going to find out. And you're going to be stopped. You hear that? You're going to be stopped."

Baylor looked briefly at Kyle, then back to Gillian, who stood next to them by the open car door.

"Maybe you haven't heard?" Baylor smiled without warmth, the blue eyes crystals of ice. "We're already past the point of no return. We're doing business here." From his pocket he pulled out one of Kyle's checks, passing it before her eyes, then, dropping the smile, drew the paper away.

"Come on, Gillian," Kyle said sternly.

She dodged the arm that would have surrounded her; he obviously intended to lead her away.

"Then you'll be put out of business. You'll be found out," she said. "And so will the others. I'll get them, too."

"Gillian..." Kyle clamped a hand on her arm. The pressure was firm, a deliberate warning that she had gone too far. She shook off his hand.

"Oh...yeah...yeah..." Baylor said, looking at her more closely. "I get it now. You're the one, huh? The lady with the big eyes and the snoopy nose. You made quite a little scene there the other day in Santa Fe. But it didn't do any good, did it?"

"Come on, Gillian." Kyle's voice rang firmly, overlapping Baylor's. "We've got things to do."

"This is what I'm doing," she said, not flinching beneath Baylor's venomous blue stare.

"Well, little lady, I'm going to tell you what you aren't going to be doing anymore." Baylor didn't move a muscle, yet Gillian had the impression her shoulders had been gripped by cold, bony fingers. "You aren't going to be poking your nose around Santa Fe anymore. Is she?" Baylor's eyes darted to Kyle.

Kyle stared back and said, "Touch her...one finger, Baylor, and I swear I'll kill you."

Something in Kyle's delivery made Baylor hesitate. Gillian could see his mind working. Then, recovering his composure, he said, "No, no...you got it all wrong, Dayton." Baylor laughed sharply. "You're the good guy, remember? We've got the other roles. A lot of the old style's gone, of course—taken over by men in three-piece suits, but a little of the old tradition's still around. That's what this movie's all about, isn't it? Tradition? The old ways? Well, they still work." And now there was no humor. His delivery was dead serious.

Baylor slipped from their company, sinking into the softly upholstered folds of the black Lincoln.

Shaken, Gillian watched the out-of-state license plate until the car had traveled out of range. "Nevada," she murmured. A small aluminum frame surrounding the state plates had advertised a Las Vegas car dealer. "Las Vegas, Nevada."

"Okay, so? Is it clear now?" Kyle asked. "You're not playing with petty bureaucrats. These aren't good old boys pushing memos around on desks. You get that finally, don't you?"

The car was only a dark, blurred stain on the horizon now.

Yes, she understood. This was outside muscle, as they said in the old black and white flicks.

"I understand who they are," she answered.

The following day, after an almost entirely sleepless night for her, and with Kyle getting his meager four hours of shut-eye, filming moved to a butte overlooking the plain that surrounded Weed Junction. The plateau offered a breathtaking view of the area, including the town of Weed Junction itself.

It also provided a view of the team of surveyors, who had returned.

Gillian heard Kyle curse to himself when the truck first appeared. It seemed hard for him to concentrate after that. And then it became impossible.

Down below, three more people had moved onto the scene. Standing on different sides of the butte, separated by extras and moviemaking equipment, Gillian and Kyle watched three old Indians walk within fifteen or twenty feet of the men who were measuring the land. John Proudfeather and his two female companions were very still. They stood like statues, patiently observing the men as they designed the thoroughfare that would eventually mark the end of their world.

Gillian felt sickened at the sight.

"Okay, break! Take the rest of the day!" Kyle called abruptly.

Gillian wasn't the only one to be shocked. Everyone else on site exchanged looks. What madness was this? It had taken them five hours to set up, and now he was ending the day's shoot?

Gillian moved to where he was standing, looking down at the men measuring the earth. "Kyle?"

He shook his head, not looking at her. "Not now, okay?"

It wasn't okay, and she was about to tell him so, but just then a production assistant approached Kyle with a stack of papers. Kyle stared through the man, not responding to what was being explained. His mind was elsewhere. "Later," he said, and started down the butte on foot, heading for the spot where his pickup truck was parked.

Before he got in, he looked back up. Gillian was watching him. They stared at each other for a long moment. Then, deliberately, he drove away without her.

Kyle clutched the wheel tightly with both hands. He saw that his knuckles were white; most likely his face had drained of color as well. He didn't know which was worse, the feel of his body dying—the pain stabbing at him like hot pokers, blinding him so that he couldn't even see what they were shooting through the camera's lens—or the knowledge that he was killing the land and killing Gillian's love.

But what chance did he have to change any of it? He didn't even have any guarantee that he was going to live long enough to finish the film. Maybe the pain would consume him, making it impossible to think.

And Gillian . . . Heaven help him, but he loved her. But now he had nothing to give her. He wasn't going to be around to love her, to protect her, to share himself with her. And now he couldn't go through any more taxing emotional scenes. He honestly didn't have the strength left, nor the time, to help her through his death. She loved him. He knew how much, too. He could feel it. But this was actually the kindest choice he could make—to distance himself little by little, to spare her from the worst that was sure to come.

He barely made it up to the hotel room before he was hit with an excruciating pain. It ripped him apart. Lightning flashed behind lids closed tightly against the burning in his gut. His fingers scrabbled for the vial that he kept in his private medical kit, and staggering to the bathroom, he leaned against the cold sink and gulped down water and a small capsule.

The pains came more frequently now. The pills in the plastic bottle were dwindling.

He lay on the bed, drained. All he could hope for was to finish his film. Everything else was completely out of his hands now. He closed his eyes.

Then the door burst open, and Gillian was there, shouting.

"Kyle! Kyle! Something's happened!"

Chapter Sixteen

The pain had receded. He could think, see, feel without the struggle of a few minutes before. Kyle pulled himself up from his prone position on the bed and stared at Gillian, his mind ricocheting from what she was saying to noting how beautiful she was in her excitement—achingly, intolerably, unfairly, gloriously beautiful.

"Like this..." Gillian said. She spun around like a dervish, arms in the air, fingers pointed to the ceiling. "It came from nowhere, Kyle! It was so strange, so...so unbelievably *weird*. But I swear to you it happened. I saw it with my own eyes—we all saw it," she stressed with passionate conviction, apparently sensing he was not accepting her tale.

Of course she was right; the story was preposterous, though obviously she believed in her version, and for her sake he tried to at least appear interested.

As she related the event, the greenish eyes with their mixture of brown were alight with inner fire, exuding an almost tangible energy throughout the room. The summer's glow had not left her face, still flushed with happiness.

"So what do you think?" she asked.

He didn't want to bring her down to reality, but it was the only thing he could do. "A dust devil—like you said."

"No...no...not *just* a dust devil." She had stopped twirling and was looking at him with mild exasperation. "You're missing the whole point. *The* dust devil. The greatest, grandest, most spectacular whirling bit of wind and sand that has ever hit this universe!" A mischievous, gay laugh burst from her as she seemed to picture the scene again in her mind.

"Okay, I'm just trying to...picture it," he said diplomatically. "There wasn't any wind, you said, and—"

"It just suddenly appeared, zooming into the site where the surveyors were. It was enormous, larger than any I've ever seen. I swear, Kyle," she rushed on excitedly, "it seemed almost intelligent. The thing was, it hit only their equipment. The crazy thing zigzagged back and forth, as if it knew exactly what it was doing. Which was—" here she paused, looking at him with large eyes full of wonder and gladness "—to utterly and completely destroy all the work those sons of bitches had done. When it finished, there were no red flags up, no stakes, and their equipment was totally demolished. Thank God it spared their trucks, or they never would have been able to get out of town." Standing at the end of the bed she looked at Kyle, waiting for his response.

"I don't know," he said, and added to appease her, "a natural phenomenon, I guess."

She shook her head from side to side. "Uh-uh. A supernatural phenomenon. Kyle, it was a miracle."

"Okay, whatever you want to call it. That doesn't change the fact that those guys'll be back."

As soon as he said it he was sorry. Her face fell. He was a bastard; why couldn't he just let her have her temporary pie-in-the-sky happiness?

"Yeah, maybe... probably," she said, and moved away.

He knew she was hurt, not by the truth, but by the simple fact that he had thrust it upon her.

He slipped off the bed, and caught up with her in the bathroom. She had splashed water onto her face, and now she stood at the sink.

"Hey," Kyle said, "I'm sorry. I popped your pretty balloon. Forgive me?"

"Yes," she said. "Of course. I was just happy about...

Well, anyway, they're gone for the time being. As you said. It was a relief, I guess. And you're right, they'll be back."

Her eyes met his in the mirror, and he read her disappointment. Privately he cursed himself again for spoiling the one meager happy moment she had managed to snatch out of a generally forlorn situation.

He wanted to say something to make everything better, but there wasn't anything. Defeated, he rested his chin lightly against her hair. It smelled faintly of flowers—feminine and clean. At least the warmth of smooth skin against him was tangible, and in spite of his depression, his body reacted with a spasm of desire.

The pain pill had taken effect. It was possible to forget—possible to want her, possible to turn her around and kiss her deeply.

Which he did.

He felt her tremble with need in his arms as their tongues entwined. "Kyle...it's been so long...I thought maybe you'd gotten tired of me. I don't know.... Without you, without this, it feels so cold—"

"Oh, no...no...Gillian. Don't say that, don't think...let's forget everything and just love. Just love. Now," he said with urgency, and his voice broke.

He carried her to the bed, and there they made love. It was not wild and abandoned, not as most times before, but it was beautiful, reverent, aware. And as their passion built, sweeping them away from their ordinary selves, they became extraordinary lovers, the feelings bursting through their skin, electrifying their lovemaking.

Kyle hadn't expected the explosiveness of their joining. When it came, it was like a shock wave expanding through his entire body. Gillian, who rode atop him, caught the jolt of ecstasy, bursting with him, crying out, unaware of the world they had left behind in that instant of complete fulfillment.

After the day of the Dust Devil Miracle, as Gillian insisted on labeling it, their relationship remained somewhat better. She consoled herself with the knowledge that Kyle's love was still there, and just as intense. Even so, it was unsettling that its external expression had altered, or more specifically, had waned.

"Guess what?" Stella said, when the three of them were dining together.

"Can't guess," Gillian said. "Pass the hot sauce, *por favor.*" She waved wiggly fingers at Stella. They were having tacos—chicken tacos in crisp tortilla shells, with lettuce and tomatoes and cheese and onions. It was a deliciously messy affair, and the high point of her low day, a day she'd mostly spent muddling over Kyle.

Stella passed the red salsa. "John Proudfeather's a shaman now."

"What?" Gillian loaded her taco with the cheery red condiment.

"A witch doctor. John's a witch doctor."

"I know... I *know* what a shaman *is*. I just don't understand, you know...." Gillian broke off, eyeing the almost empty bowl of guacamole dip. To Kyle she said, "I know this is perfectly evil, but do you think we could get more?"

"Can your conscience live with it?" Kyle asked with a meaningful sweep of his eyes along the length of her body.

"It's my thighs I'm mostly worried about," Gillian returned. "But I can handle the anguish."

Kyle caught the attention of one of the kitchen staff and made the request.

"Anyway," Gillian said, "what I mean is, what makes you say this about John?" She bit into the taco, squeezing lettuce and tomatoes and cheese out the sides, while the sauce dripped down to her wrists.

Stella shook her head in disgust, but resumed her story. "The dust devil the other day—the humongous, whirling sandstorm? John claims it was his doing." Stella nodded, then giggled. "Can you believe it! The man's too much. You know, he's cute, really cute. He truly believes in himself. Have you seen him lately? He's so...I don't know...dignified all of a sudden."

Kyle seemed not to hear what they were saying. His eyes appeared cloudy. Now accustomed to such moods, Gillian left him alone. Maybe, she rationalized, all directors and producers got this way.

The comparative peace in their lives was brought to an end two days later when the bulldozers appeared. For an entire day they gouged the land, scraping and shoving earth that had been in place for centuries. Filming continued, but in the background, the steady hum of the earth-moving machinery was a constant and cruel reminder of a fate that was fast bearing down on them.

Even when engrossed in his directorial duties, Kyle looked stricken.

And seeing him in such torment, Gillian felt a tight band of anxiety closing around her own chest. Mobsters or not, she had to do something.

And then the second miracle occurred, this one in the form of a sudden, freak desert storm—a cloudburst that left Kyle's site untouched, but which washed out the road-grading work.

In the aftermath of the fifteen-minute deluge, Stella sidled up to Gillian, whispering, "Score one for John."

"Yeah, sure . . ." said Gillian absently, as, standing on the high dry ground, she looked below to the scene of the flood.

"No, I'm serious." Stella giggled. "Before it happened, he told me he was going to do it. Honestly."

Gillian looked at Stella and shook her head.

"Hey . . . listen, city girl, there's a lot that goes on out here that is just plain weird and spooky. No normal explanations handle some things."

"Except when people are sober."

Later in their hotel room, Gillian said glumly to Kyle, "I'd really like to believe it. I'd love to believe in all that magic stuff. At least we'd have a sporting chance with a bunch of gods on our side."

As usual he wore a preoccupied expression, but now he at least had an excuse. He was sitting at the edge of the bed, figuring on his calculator. "Yeah, well . . . after enough beers, I guess you can have all the gods you'd ever want playing on your team."

Gillian left the dresser and settled on the bed, her back against the headboard and knees pulled up to her chest. "Still, it's nice to think about."

"Why play mind games? It's just a matter of time and they'll be back with their machines." With that he punched out a series of numbers.

She wanted to believe that he was only being his recent negative self. But two hours later she found out how wrong she was and how right Kyle had been.

The enemy had returned to Weed Junction.

Gillian left Kyle to add up his numbers and decided to walk down the road to John Proudfeather's, thinking to celebrate with him the good news of the flood. Temporary or not, it had been another obstacle in the enemy's path; and that was worth at least a spot of good cheer.

Only John Proudfeather's place wasn't there. Where it *had* been there was now a rank-smelling, smoldering heap of debris.

Gillian found Pablita poking around in the ashes and coals and melted muck of plastic household items, searching for anything that might have remained intact. Her face had trails of dark smudges, as if smoky tears had fallen from her eyes.

Pablita said the trailer had gone up like a tinderbox. In less than a half hour, the metal and wood box that had been John's home for so many years had been completely consumed by the flames. She and Maria had only barely managed to save John, who had been knocked unconscious by a falling structural support as he attempted to fight his way to the front door to escape the inferno.

Gillian asked to see him, and was led into the one-room adobe house, where John had been placed on a narrow sofa and was being ministered to by Maria with herbal treatments and chanting. A thin stream of sage incense burning in a blue bowl spiraled toward the ceiling, filling the air with a fresh sweetness.

"How did it happen?" Gillian asked.

"You must ask him," said Pablita. "When he wakes."

Gillian waited with the two Indian women, who took turns in placing compresses on John's burns. She even hummed along with the chants, finding the tones soothing. Dark came, and the women lighted candles. The light jumped and danced as if there were a breeze in the closed room. Three hours passed before John was conscious again.

"How, John? How did it happen? Did you leave a pot on the stove?" She was thinking that she would have to see about having him move in with the women so they could watch over him. Senility was a factor in so many senseless tragedies.

But when John spoke, it was with lucid awareness. If anything, as Stella had said, his words seemed more cogent than ever.

Two men from Nevada were responsible for the fire, he said. A couple of the road crew were Indians. They had laughed to themselves after having seen John and Maria and Pablita in the area, knowing that they were up to their magic. They had even said as much to the foreman. The foreman had only laughed the first time, but too many things were going wrong on this project—things that couldn't be explained by any normal means. He was starting to look bad. There were big things and little things that kept happening that wrecked the job they had been hired to do. The head of the project needed someone to blame. He needed to stop whatever was making things go wrong for him, so he picked on John as the scapegoat. He hired some men to set fire to the trailer, meaning to scare the magic out of John and his two Indian accomplices.

"How did you know all of this?"

From an Indian woman whose son was on the road crew, Pablita said. The woman came by the day before and warned them about the gossip. But the dan-

ger didn't make any difference, said Maria with proud
confidence; they were going to perform their magic,
no matter what. The spirits of their ancestors were
with them, and the gods of nature had gathered to as-
sist in their enterprise.

Gillian stared incredulous.

John must have picked up her thoughts from her
expression.

"It's fine that you don't believe," he said. "I didn't
either. At first. It isn't a question of belief. It's knowing for your own self that matters. It takes work.
Magic's not easy."

He told her that after Gillian had arrived in Weed
Junction and had been so insistent about them having
to have something to share with her for posterity, he
had started to think. He felt bad that he was going to
be leaving the earth without ever having known his
own heritage. So he thought he would give it one last
try—actually it was both a first and a last try. He
racked his brains for what he remembered of the old
ways of his grandfathers, and he stole a little here and
there from what he knew of the magic made by some
of the other tribes he had visited. Then he set to work.
Maybe it was because he was so old that the gods
graced him with so much potency, but almost immediately he found himself gaining success in his en-
deavors. The bell, John claimed, was rung that day to
awaken the spirits that had been sleeping in the church
of San Geronimo. He had invited his ancestors to join
in his education, putting on the owl costume to draw
them into his realm. The dust devil had been a
breathtaking success, of course, but he had done a lot

of little miracles first, all private trials leading up to the storm.

"That was good, wasn't it?" he chuckled softly in spite of his obvious physical discomfort. "That was really something."

"That was something, all right," Gillian agreed.

"I was born to follow this course," John explained. "I was supposed to be a man of knowledge, of healing. But I was silly and wasted myself. I used to be afraid." He smiled and looked at Gillian with his bright, dark eyes. "You know about that," he said.

He told her that the secret of power was to align oneself with the forces of nature, to become one with them. Then all the nature gods were your allies, and as long as you worked for good, they would come to your aid.

Although she respected him, Gillian shook her head. "These guys, John, they don't really understand about the magic. They deal in their own kind of magic—guns. They almost killed you today."

John listened, his dark glittering eyes intent on what she said. He seemed almost excited by the threatening situation, possibly even amused. "And what will you do to stop them?"

"Me?" Gillian looked at him. "I tried, but—"

"I guess you didn't try hard enough."

"There's nothing left for me to do."

"There's always a way," John said.

"I can't get to see the governor."

"If you can't get in a door, you try a window. If you can't get in a window, you come down the chimney. If there isn't a chimney, you walk through the walls." And then, suddenly seeming exhausted, his eyes closed and his voice faded into a deep, regular breathing pattern.

Walk through the walls. The preposterous phrase was repeated in Gillian's mind the whole night and continued the following morning until she couldn't stand it anymore. It was a fact that if she wanted to see the governor, she was probably going to have to walk through walls, because no one was about to let her in any other way.

Kyle rose early as usual, leaving her to have breakfast on her own. She invited Stella to join her. Stella wasn't a great deal of company; she kept her nose stuck in the newspaper, reading a piece of gossip about an American woman who had married a sheikh and was suing him for divorce, including two hundred million dollars.

"See," Stella said, "this babe's got the right idea. You could learn a thing or two from her about your marital rights. In case you ever decide to...hey!"

Gillian had snatched the paper from Stella. There on the front page was an announcement of a press conference to be given by the governor late that afternoon.

Here was her opportunity. She was going to walk through the walls and yell her head off when she got to the other side.

Chapter Seventeen

She wasn't in the habit of praying, not formally anyway. But that day she did.

It didn't matter that she wasn't Catholic; the church of San Geronimo seemed welcoming to her just the same. For a few minutes, she sat on one of the hard wooden pews. She closed her eyes tightly and asked for help.

She was afraid, but she had to do it; she couldn't walk away from herself. It just wasn't possible.

Fifteen minutes later she rose from the hard bench and made her way through the small, silent church. Just before leaving, she turned and looked back inside, her eyes searching the shadows for a sign that there was someone or something there to hear her. But it was just a quiet room; nothing stirred but the hard beat of her frightened heart, and without any hope of supernatural assistance, she pushed her way through the door into the fall sunlight.

She was lost in thought and didn't see Kyle coming forward as she passed from the courtyard, through the high white stucco arch and onto the street. He grabbed her by the shoulders, startling her from her reverie.

"Stella told me," he said. "Are you serious? I can't believe you're going to be so stupid—"

"I have to go," Gillian said, pulling herself from his arms.

But he caught her and pressed her against him, holding her as he spoke. "Why?" he objected violently. "They won't listen to you."

"John's not going to stop," Gillian said, again pulling away. "He was almost burned to death, and he's still going to fight them. But he can't. He's nothing but an old, partially crazy...no, let's just say deluded man. But he's a good person, and I feel responsible. If I hadn't come here and given him all these notions of how honorable and brave the native American man is, then maybe he never would have started to meddle in things that are totally over his head. If I can do anything, I will. I owe him that much. He could be killed, Kyle. You're absolutely right. Those guys weren't messing around."

"No kidding."

"At least you can't call me naive anymore."

"No, not naive. You're way past that, a long, long way down the road. I'd say you're all the way into reckless now. Anyway, you won't even be able to get in," Kyle said matter-of-factly, as if he had just pulled out the secret winning card.

"Getting in's no problem. It's already arranged," she said, pleased to be able to show him how thorough she had been. "There'll be a pass waiting for me at the door. I'm going as an observer, a visiting scholar. The director of the museum vouched for me, pulled some strings."

"Then do everyone a favor and unarrange all the arrangements," Kyle replied angrily.

"You know I can't."

"I know that you're going to get yourself killed."

"I understand what I'm doing. Anyway, why do you think I dressed so nicely today? Dead or alive, if I make headlines, no one's going to say I'm dowdy. Compliments of Stella," Gillian said, and twirled to show herself off.

Stella had loaned her a fitted lavender dress, which Gillian wore with navy heels. Also thrown in were Stella's small gold earrings.

But it seemed that Kyle wasn't interested in fashion statements. "Gillian, for God's sake, be sensible. This isn't Vista del Bravo. It's gone too far for speeches. The men are in already. They've won."

But it didn't make any difference to her what he said, and of course he knew it. In the end, Kyle accompanied her to the Mustang.

"You're doing the retake of your big scene today, huh?" she said, looking up at him through the open window as she sat behind the wheel.

He nodded absently. "Don't go."

"I wish I could be here to see it. You make a terrific lone cowboy hero," she said. "Really," and she touched the hand rested on the door.

Then, before he could change her mind, she started the Mustang and pulled away,.

After that, Kyle found it hard to concentrate. He would have liked to go after her. But the scene was perhaps the most important in the entire film, and he had to stay in Weed Junction.

The lighting was perfect. He couldn't have asked anything more from Mother Nature, who had blessed him with a perfectly clear blue sky. It was what he had wanted, how he had seen the scene in his mind—a lonely, barren street, the world stripped down to its essence with just one good man standing against evil.

They were just set to shoot when the sounds of the giant tractors intruded again. *Back, they were back.* He imagined huge dragons ripping away at the earth.

"Okay, let's have at it," Kyle said, and everyone took their positions.

The cameras were rolling, the actors saying their lines. Soon it would be his cue. He tried not to think of the machinery. He tried not to think of Gillian.

Kyle got into position for his entrance. In three more lines he would leave his role of director and become Kyle the movie star.

And he was on.

The lines came automatically; he knew every part, every nuance of every character. It wasn't the final scene they would shoot, but it was the final scene of the movie that the audience would see. It had to ring true.

He was the quiet, lone hero who had ridden into town, the mysterious stranger who had cleaned up the corruption. Right now he was saying goodbye to the woman he had come to love while he was there fighting against injustice. He didn't want to go, but he had to. That was the kind of man he was—principle over passion.

The actress was saying her lines perfectly. And he was doing his own part to absolute perfection. He was totally into it. Because every word he was saying was the way he wished it could be. And the better he was at his part, the sicker he felt inside.

The cameras kept rolling.

As called for in the script, he turned suddenly from the woman and lifted himself onto the horse. Without looking back, he rode down the center of Weed Junction, the way it would have looked back in the late eighteen hundreds.

The camera was following his movement through the street. Down the lonely road he trotted, looking straight ahead, and then, as he passed the church of San Geronimo, the bells began to peal slowly, just as called for in the script.

A camera was at the end of the road, facing him dead ahead. There was a close-up coming up, a close-up of his face, and he was supposed to show strength and stony resolve.

Only he wasn't.

He was crying. He couldn't stop the tears. Coming one after the other, they fell almost in time to the bell's chiming. He remembered the bell that first morning he had met Gillian.

God, what was happening? He was ruining the shot. But he couldn't stop the tears. The bell kept tolling, he kept riding, and the tears kept coming. And then a voice cried out—the voice of the assistant director who was behind the cameraman, closing in on his face for the final frame. "Cut! Cut!"

The director was walking forward, looking disturbed. "You want to go over that last part again. It was great really, right up until the bells. But we had it worked out so you were the rough-tough loner with a job to do, and instead..." The man looked embarrassed. "The tears—they weren't the way we planned."

Kyle was looking at the man, but his mind was cutting in and out of the conversation. "The scene stays," Kyle said abruptly.

"With the tears?"

"Yeah. The tears work. That's just how the guy would have felt."

The press conference was at four that afternoon. Gillian wound her way through the crowded anteroom and found the table where her visitor's pass was held. Pinning it onto herself, she got inside the pressroom without any trouble and took a seat about two-thirds of the way from the podium.

There were cameras and wires and lights and a lot of banter and jockeying for position. A large number of reporters sat in chairs like hers, waiting for the program to begin.

Then suddenly everything was quiet.

The governor entered and moved with stately elegance to the large raised podium. She felt as if she were in the presence of The Great Oz. He gave his speech amid a circus of whirring and popping and humming and whining mechanical and electronic instruments. Gillian was too nervous to hear anything he said. He looked fine, cool as the proverbial cucumber. She kept rehearsing her own speech. But sometimes she couldn't even remember her first word. Her throat was becoming excruciatingly dry. She wondered if she would even be able to squeak, much less inspire confidence with her oratory. Something dreadful was going on in her stomach. Her breathing was becoming more rapid. Her heart was going like a motor on a self-destruct mission. There was no strength in any of her limbs.

Now she saw that the governor was smiling. There was a great wave of applause. The governor was smiling in her direction. Was he looking at her? she thought in panic. Had he called her name? No. No. She had to calm down. The governor had simply finished his speech, and now was open to questions from the floor.

She had questions. That was why she had come here—to ask her questions and to tell them a few things, as well.

She was going to be sick.

The printed agenda in her hand said that there were fifteen minutes set aside for reporters to quiz the governor. A glance at her watch showed that there were only three minutes remaining of the fifteen. How was that possible?

Then there were only two minutes left.

She wanted to die.

There was one minute left. She had to do it, had to....

And then she had raised her hand. No, her hand had raised *her*. The governor was looking at her. And so was everyone else. Everyone was waiting. Even she was waiting.

Another man broke in. Rising, he began to ask his question.

That made her mad, reminding her of Vista del Bravo, where she had been cast aside as though she didn't exist.

Above the man's voice, her own rang out with force. "Mr. Governor...Mr. Governor...I have knowledge that your administration is rife with criminal activity. Mr. Governor, I have proof with me that will show that..."

All eyes turned toward her now, some mouths agape. And it was okay. A sense of control possessed her.

"I can show that—"

But another voice covered hers. From behind her, a masculine voice overpowered hers. "She risked her life coming here today to be heard."

Suddenly the eyes were no longer on her. Everyone in the room, herself included, had fixed their attention on Kyle Dayton, the famous movie star, the legend in his own time who was moving down the central aisle of the room with three old Indians following closely behind.

The press conference lasted much longer than had been anticipated. Kyle and Gillian couldn't name names. But Kyle did have a check that had been cashed, and photocopies of it were passed around for any of the press who might like to trace the endorser's name. Kyle also had a lot of suspicions that became public knowledge.

"By your wide smiles and shiny eyes, I'm assuming some of you will be delighted to uncover some of this information that certain others would prefer to keep covered." There was explosive laughter at Kyle's sly remark.

While the flashbulbs popped, Gillian smiled through her tears at Kyle and John Proudfeather, who flanked her, one on either side, the two Indian women standing slightly off center, shying away from the cameras. She squeezed the men's fingers, and they each squeezed her hand back. She thought she saw a tear glistening in John Proudfeather's eye, but how could she tell for sure? She was laughing and crying too hard to tell.

The next three days were busy ones. Kyle was interviewed by the national media and by people on a special committee formed to look into the allegations he and Gillian had set forth. Gillian was interviewed as well. And John Proudfeather, especially, had a lot of things to say. He claimed to have saved them up for his whole life, which was longer than anyone else's around. He had things to say about Indians in general, and about the land in particular. So for three days they were five happy heroes.

And then the circus was over.

Only Gillian didn't know it. She was so happy, so overjoyed that Kyle had come to support her, that she had completely forgotten what the time away from the film had cost Kyle personally.

It had cost him everything. He was over budget. There was enough to pay the actors and technicians, and barely enough to complete filming. But the rest of it, the editing, the marketing and distribution—none of the postproduction expenses could be covered.

"I'm sorry," she said when she discovered the truth about his situation. "Kyle, I'm so sorry—"

"Don't be. It was my decision. Something I had to do."

"For me."

"Yes. And also for me. And being sorry doesn't change anything. We did some good, anyway. The land will remain untouched, at least for the time being."

"And when your film is distributed, there'll be others who will eventually carry the torch," she said.

Kyle didn't say anything.

"The film's going to make it, isn't it? I mean, somehow?"

"Yeah," he said after a long pause. But it wasn't said with any conviction, and when Gillian tried to pursue the matter, he froze her out.

There weren't any opportunities after that to discuss the matter. He seemed constantly distracted, and if she thought he had been cold before, that was nothing.

So she was left to brood over matters on her own. There wasn't anything more for her to do on the film, and that left her with a lot of time—too much time—on her hands.

John Proudfeather thought he had a solution to her problem. He was now a reborn Indian and was forever after her to write his memoirs. He had become an instant celebrity, receiving letters from all over the country from people who had read about him in the papers and seen him on television. Shamans, it appeared, were currently the rage. He was terribly insistent about his book.

"I can't, John."

"You aren't doing anything else," he said.

"Yes, I am. I'm worrying. Worrying takes up a lot of time and energy."

"That's stupid. You write my book, and you'll learn my secrets on how not to worry—or at least how to worry efficiently."

"You're a psychologist, too?"

"I'm everything."

"Sometime, okay? Maybe later. Not now."

"It's always now," he said. "That's one of my secrets."

Well, *now* stank as far as she was concerned. *Now* was when Kyle was barely civil to her. He was increasingly vague about their future and no longer interested in making love at all. Then, just when she would almost give up and get ready to pack her bags and leave, he would do something, say something, and for an instant he would be as tender and connected with her as ever he had been in the past. There was an added intensity to him that hadn't been there before. When he laughed, it was with a full abandon that made her wonder if it was truly laughter and not an expression of sorrow. But the fact remained that for three weeks, he didn't touch her.

"I don't understand," Gillian railed one night after Kyle turned away from her again.

"I'm tired," he said wearily. "Please, Gillian, let's talk about this tomorrow."

"You're punishing me," she said, unwilling to be put off again. "You didn't have to come to my rescue. You chose to—and so you lost money. And now, now you're blaming me."

The words she had spoken struck Kyle's ears like brutal thunder. He was dying, and in the interim he was slowly killing the woman he loved.

He couldn't tell her. If he did, she would pity him. Not telling her, of course, was selfishness on his part; he wanted her to remember him as he was. She would suffer far more if she hung on for the whole trip to the funeral home. Cancer wasn't pretty; the victim didn't die nicely. He didn't want her to go through that horror. The tubes and masks and needles. For him, all the ugliness was inevitable, and the most he could hope for was to die with a little grace. At least there would be the painkillers, so eventually he wouldn't feel anything. His brain would kick off.

But hers wouldn't. Gillian would suffer.

The pain pill he had taken only a few hours before was wearing off. He had only ten left in the vial, and he was beginning to panic. He had some loose ends to tie up in the film, and then he would be free to take off for L.A. where he could get a new prescription, once he had seen the doctor.

Even as he planned the future, a searing pain ripped through him. He needed another pill, needed to hide the pain from Gillian.

A second pain sliced through him. Leaving the bed, he made it into the bathroom, shut the door and grabbed the small vial of pain medicine from his toiletry kit on the counter. It would take a few minutes for it to take effect. He waited, holding onto the counter, feeling weak, feeling confused, feeling alone and very terrified.

"Kyle?" Gillian was on the other side of the door, her voice full of questions he couldn't answer.

"Kyle?" she asked again, more insistently now. "Are you okay?"

I'm dying, Gillian. And you're only making it worse for me, because I love you and I don't want you to see me die. "Yeah." He gripped the sink as another pain tore at him. "Everything's okay."

"I don't believe you."

"Listen! Listen to me! Will you just get off my back? Could you do that for me, Gillian?" Shouting had almost done him in. The exertion had cost him dearly. His entire stomach felt like a raw piece of meat. He was crying—because of the pain; because of what he was doing to Gillian.

She didn't say anything more, and he felt like hell. He shouldn't have been so brutal. It was the pain. When he went back to bed he'd hold her. After the pill took effect, things would be better and they could talk. Maybe he was wrong to keep things from her. Maybe he would tell her. Yes, maybe that was the right thing to do after all.

More than ten minutes had passed. The pain was gone. He splashed some water onto his face, then opened the door and, stepping into the darkened bedroom, said with as much grace as he could, "I'm sorry... I shouldn't have talked to you like that." The bathroom had been brightly lighted, and he had to refocus for the dark. "Gillian, I love you. It's because I love you, I've been acting so stiff—so cold." He was almost at the bed. "There's some bad news, I'm afraid, but maybe we should talk about it, anyway."

He stood by the bed, looking down, and the dark was no longer a problem. He could see clearly.

Gillian wasn't there anymore.

Chapter Eighteen

She hadn't packed much. Until she got to California, she didn't even know what she had taken. The rest of the things would be sent for when she got settled. Stella would do that for her.

"I'm going back to California," she had said to Stella, standing outside her apartment door.

Stella had nodded. "I guess you know what you're doing this time."

"I guess I do."

"Hey," Stella called, just as Gillian was stepping outside. Gillian looked back. "You've come a long way, city girl."

"Too long, Stella—way, way too long. I don't know if I'll ever be able to find my way home again." And then she stepped into the night where the moon was a sliver, gleaming like a sharp sickle that was ripping heaven apart.

She didn't cry once on the drive back to Los Angeles. She just kept her eye on the road and her mind a blank. If she shed one tear, she would drown herself in ten million. She'd never stop. Not ever. So deep was her grief.

When she got to Barstow, she stopped at a pay phone at a gas station and called her friend, Carol. Carol taught at U.C. Santa Barbara. She had a little house near the coast, a frame cottage surrounded by tropical plants, which made it seem removed from the rest of the world. That was what Gillian wanted—to be removed. Gillian was welcomed warmly. "Stay as long as you like. Or need to," Carol said, apparently responding to something in Gillian's voice.

"She's gone."

Kyle faced Stella in her apartment. She wore a silver Mylar jumpsuit with rhinestones imbedded in starburst designs on the top. Her high-heeled boots were also silver with the same rhinestone motif.

"I know she's gone. That's why I'm here. Because she's gone, and I don't know where."

"I don't know, either. Really. Really, I don't," she repeated. "You're hurting bad, huh?"

"Somewhat," Kyle said acidly, not because he was angry at Stella or even doubted her, but out of frustration.

"I like that in a man," said Stella.

"Pain?"

"Yeah, kind of. Sometimes I think it's only women who get hurt. You never, hardly ever, see any real guy suffer."

"You're seeing one now," said Kyle, walking out.

John Proudfeather wasn't any more help than Stella. In fact, he seemed really upset when Kyle stopped by the adobe house to talk to him.

"She didn't say goodbye," John said. "Doesn't make any sense." He shook his head, thinking about it. Then he brightened. "Because she's coming back. We've got a book to do."

Kyle left him with his illusions. But he knew better; Gillian had left Weed Junction for good.

And after three more days, so did Kyle.

When he got to L.A. he had one pill left. There was no postponing the crucial visit to the doctor. He went to the same specialist who had helped him through the first round with the disease.

The doctor's face looked as grave as the one Kyle figured he'd be lying in before long. The symptoms were duly recorded, and amid a lot of "Hmm"'s and "Umm"'s and inscrutable nods, the doctor advised Kyle that he would have to go into the hospital for tests. There would be the exploratory surgery and a biopsy, just as before.

"I'm sorry," the doctor said. "It doesn't look good."

"It doesn't feel good, either," Kyle quipped. Nothing like one's own impending demise to turn one into a lighthearted raconteur.

"The pills will help," said the doctor, handing him a prescription. "You check into the hospital tomorrow."

"Make it the next day. I've got something I've got to do first."

"But—"

"Hey...I can die a day later, is all. This *can't* wait."

Gordon Millman was as surprised to see Kyle as Kyle was surprised to find himself walking into Millman's office. A couple of years ago, he would have considered such a scene an impossibility.

The moment he saw Millman, Kyle was glad he had come. He loved the man. Even if he was one of the worst bastards in the business and had done everything but rip Kyle's heart out with his bare hands, Kyle felt an affinity for the guy. Love was more than blind; it was sometimes downright perverse.

"So," Millman said, not rising from behind his large rosewood desk. "I understand you finished your shoot-em-up. Nothing personal, but you look like hell, Dayton. Clean air'll kill you. Want a cigarette?"

"No thanks, I'm dying just fine on my own steam." It was his own private little joke. Naturally Millman didn't get it.

When the barbs had been fired back and forth, Kyle stated his reason for coming by. He handed the can of film to Millman and said, "Tell me what you think. If you like it, then I need an investor to finish off the editing and see that it gets the proper distribution."

"What? You crazy? You know I'm the enemy." Millman fitted the part well. He was of medium height, with an angular face gone fleshy in age, giving him the air of a bloated hawk. Once he had been almost attractive; Kyle had seen photographs of him as a younger man. The eyes were still bright, but appeared smaller within the extra folds of skin. He dressed impeccably, each of his shirts costing as much as many middle-management executives earned in a week, and on his wrist a diamond-encrusted Rolex flashed its brilliance like a sign over a Las Vegas casino.

"You're also the best. Or so you say," Kyle said, and both men laughed a little. "You may not have had the vision to make this epic masterpiece, but maybe you'll have the heart to enjoy it. You could also stand to make a bundle." Kyle rose from the upholstered swivel chair he had taken across from Millman's desk. Looking down at his former mentor, Kyle said, "Look at it this way, Gordon. I'm giving you a chance to do something for yourself that's good."

"You're one arrogant bastard, Dayton!" Millman slapped his hand on the table, then sank back into his chair, nodding. "And you used to be such a nice kid. Hollywood sure can spoil a man."

"You said it, pal."

"Show yourself out, kid. I've got business to do. Big business. And you're wasting my time."

Gillian was in Santa Barbara when she heard the news on the television. Kyle Dayton, the announcer said, had checked into a Los Angeles hospital for a medical biopsy for cancer. Reports were that he had been previously diagnosed as having the disease, but had, after surgery and postoperative therapy, re-covered. Mention was made of Kyle's professional background, but Gillian didn't hear any of it.

Her heart uttered a long, silent scream—the wail filled her soul. No! No! Not Kyle! Not her Kyle!

And then, in a lucid flash of understanding, everything became clear to her. He had been sick, that was why he had turned from her. But why hadn't he told her?

She felt guilty and sorrowful and angry, all at the same time. Why hadn't he shared himself with her? How could he think he was going to die on her now? She wouldn't let him get away with it. This was one fight she was going to win.

They wouldn't let her see Kyle when she arrived at the hospital. They told her he had been sedated so that he would get a good night's sleep before the surgery in the morning. She argued. They remained firm. They were apparently used to seeing crazed women.

She raged a bit more, but it was no use. There would be no visitors in Kyle Dayton's room, and that was final. The woman was tough, experienced. She said she'd already turned away about twenty reporters. Gillian saw there was a bunch of cards and boxes and flower arrangements put in a corner nearby. They would be for Kyle.

So she sat in the waiting room instead. She would not leave him. If it only meant that she could share the same roof with him, she would do that. She would never leave Kyle again.

She had nodded off, and when she looked up, responding to the sound of her name, she thought she was still dreaming.

Standing before her were John Proudfeather and Maria Trujillo and Pablita Morningstar. John was carrying a large burlap sack with him, giving him the appearance of a destitute Santa. There were only four other people in the waiting room, but they seemed too preoccupied with their own problems to pay much notice to a few Indians.

"What are you doing here?" Gillian asked in wonder.

"Come on," said John, starting off again, "we've got work to do."

Indian stealth wasn't just a myth. Led by John, the four of them crept down the hall without being apprehended by any of the ordinarily vigilant nurses. Twice Gillian thought they were about to be nabbed, but instead the members of the hospital staff walked past them as if they were invisible.

One after the other they checked each room and finally lucked out, locating Kyle's. It had a big sign on it reading, Private—No Admittance. They entered and closed the door quietly. Gillian wanted to run to Kyle, who was sleeping soundly beneath white sheets and covers, but John stopped her.

"No time," he said. "We're going to work now."

In the bag John carried were a lot of strange things. John pulled out the items one by one. There was a feathered headdress, a touch mangy-looking as if it had been bought in a secondhand store, but when placed on John's head, Gillian had to admit it took on a certain flair. Then came a long pipe and some rocks, which John arranged in the shape of a wheel with spokes coming out from the center.

Gillian didn't have to ask to know that the circle signified eternal life; that was elementary for an anthropologist. It was a medicine wheel used in sacred healing ceremonies.

Sage incense was lighted, and Gillian was told to position herself at the end of a pie-shaped wedge formed by the rocks; the others likewise took their own positions. The chanting began. It was soft, but fervent.

Gillian didn't know the words and couldn't follow the atonal melody. Instead, she prayed with all her heart that Kyle would be all right. *Take away his sickness, leave him whole and mine to love forever,* she prayed.

Sometime later, John tapped her on the shoulder and said softly, "It's okay now."

She felt light-headed, almost happy. She wasn't aware of having fallen asleep, but perhaps she had. The medicine wheel was gone, packed away in the bag. The only sign that a ritual had been performed was the lingering smell of the incense.

Gillian rose, her eyes going to Kyle, who still slept soundly.

"Time to go," John said, pulling her with him. The two Indian women were waiting for him by the door. "The spirits are here now. They'll do the rest."

Gillian was still in the waiting room at 10:00 a.m., when Kyle was wheeled out of Recovery and into his private room. She still wasn't allowed in to see him. He was going to be under medication for a long time.

The nurse suggested she go home and rest. Gillian said she'd wait.

She didn't know what had become of John and Maria and Pablita. It had never occurred to her that they would leave, but they must have. They were nowhere to be found. It made sense, though: the three were prone to appearing and disappearing whenever the time was right.

When Kyle awoke slightly after noon, she was allowed to visit.

"Hey," she said, smiling and trying not to cry as she slipped into the room.

He turned his head to the doorway. For a second he didn't say anything but only looked at her. Then he too said, "Hey." It hardly sounded like him.

"I don't want to tire you out," she said, "but on the other hand, wild horses couldn't drag me away. Oh, Kyle..." She crossed the room rapidly to stand by his bed. She reached for him and held his hand gently. Biting her lip in an effort to keep back the tears that were already gathering, she said, "I didn't know. If only I had known—"

"I know. My mistake. Not yours. I didn't want you to go through this," he said. He sounded far away, as if even now he was leaving her.

"Go through what? Loving you and not being with you?"

"I don't know if I'm going to make it, Gillian."

"What? Are you crazy? Sure you're going to make it...of course you're going to make it." She thought she sounded hysterical, as if she were battling unseen demons.

"I can't believe you're here," Kyle said, his eyes drinking her in. "I thought I'd never see you again. How'd you—?"

"Sorry. It was on the television. The whole world knows. You're probably going to have to spend the rest of your life writing thank-you notes. There's a mountain of gifts and mail and flowers out there."

"I might not get around to all of them."

"Don't say that."

"I've got to. And you've got to accept it. Let's not pretend. Please . . . it'll only make it harder. I've lived a lie for so long now. And I've missed you. . . ."

She laid her head on his hand, the tears flowing copiously, running between his fingers, smearing her cheeks with wetness. "Okay . . . whatever you say. . . ." They were quiet together for a moment. Then Gillian lifted her head and said, "I can't do it. I'm sorry, but I'm not able to think you're going to die. If you think it's over . . . then you do. But I'm not going down without a fight."

"It's my fight."

"No. Not anymore. Not any more than getting up and talking in Santa Fe was my own battle. You were there for me. And so were John and Pablita and Maria." She stopped. "They came last night."

"Here?"

Gillian nodded. "I couldn't believe it. They just appeared."

"Oh . . . I wish I would have known."

"They did a ceremony for you." Gillian told him about the incense and the chanting, about the medicine wheel and the pipe.

Kyle smiled a little, clearly amused by their primitive, but well-meaning efforts. "Where are they now? I'd like to see them, to thank them."

"I don't know. They're gone. They left some spirits to watch over you, though." She smiled. "John said you're going to be okay."

"John . . ." Kyle smiled.

"Yeah, John . . . anyway, he means well."

Gillian refused to leave after the ten minutes the nurse had allotted her for visiting time.

"You'll have to take me out kicking and screaming," she said. "And that'll only upset your patient."

She was still there when the doctor arrived. Kyle and she turned their heads toward the door as it opened. She took Kyle's hand into hers and squeezed. "It's okay," she whispered, not to him, but to herself.

Her heart sank. The doctor's face didn't look as though anything was okay.

Kyle saw the physician's expression, too. His fingers grew cold in her hand, and she felt him tense slightly. She tightened her hold, as if fearing he might slip away.

The doctor gave Gillian a harsh, questioning look. "I'm going to have to talk to my patient now. Alone, if you don't mind."

"That's okay. I'm staying," she said.

"Gillian, maybe it would be better if you—"

"No! I'm staying here. I'm staying with you. Anyway, everything's going to be all right."

"Gillian—"

"Look," she said to the doctor, "I don't care what the odds are—this man is not going to die."

"I think you're—"

"Too optimistic? No. I'm not too optimistic. I'm positive—that's totally different. This man is going to live. We'll fight it. We'll fight it and we're going to win, dammit!" She was weeping, not even knowing it.

The doctor waited until she had calmed down.

"Well, then," he said, a strange look coming over his face, "I presume you'll be willing to help this man fight the urge to eat spicy food. This man has an ulcer—a very severe one. And surgery will be necessary. There's discomfort involved, and of course some risk, but it's minimal. There's always risk involved in surgery—we're required by law to explain that. But I can assure you, if I can use any of my tricks, he'll be up and around and causing hearts to throb within a few weeks' time."

On the way out the doctor turned and said, "I will tell you, though—I was surprised. Everything pointed to—well, you know. I would have staked my entire career on it being cancer. But I guess I was wrong. It's good to be wrong sometimes," he said, and for the first time he smiled warmly. Opening the door he turned again, sniffed and asked, "What's that funny smell?"

"Oh, that," said Gillian. "Spirits, I think."

He looked at her for an instant, not understanding. "Well, I don't know where they come from. I keep telling them we've got to spray these rooms."

That evening, a pie was delivered to the hospital. Gillian was there to open the box. An envelope had been stuck into the center of the pie, from which one slice was already missing. She handed Kyle the envelope, and he pulled free a card.

Kyle Dayton—you son of a gun... I send to you one humble pie, minus the piece that I have already eaten with great relish. Enclosed is a contract. As you can see, I plan on gouging you for fifty-one percent ownership of *Due West*. But what the hell—name your price. We can quibble over percentage points later, when I'm not so weighted down by pie.

P.S. Oh, and by the way, I cried at the end of the

film. I haven't cried in years—not since I was ten. Thanks.

"He loves you," Gillian said, smiling.

"Yeah." Kyle laughed. "I know. And for a man who claims he has no heart, that's some trick."

"So now that *Due West* is guaranteed to be a blockbuster, and you're guaranteed not to kick the bucket, you've got some major time on your hands."

Kyle nodded. "Looks that way." Then he said, "I've got this new vision. It's kind of far out, but I don't know, maybe it would work. What do you think about a film where a major motion picture star meets a beautiful woman on a dirt road in the middle of nowhere and falls in love?"

"I can see it," said Gillian with a smile, squinting as if looking into the future.

"And maybe they fight and make up—and then they get married."

Gillian's eyes opened wide. "Really?"

"Really," Kyle said, reaching for her hand. "And then—the way it plays is, they live happily ever after."

"Yeah," said Gillian, biting her lip and trying not to cry. "I like the concept. I really like it a lot. You know, it's got big, oh...major...potential."

"Let's go for it," Kyle said.

"Let's," she agreed.

* * * * *

Diana Palmer brings you the
second Award of Excellence title
SUTTON'S WAY

In Diana Palmer's bestselling Long, Tall Texans trilogy, you had a mesmerizing glimpse of Quinn Sutton—a mean, lean Wyoming wildcat of a man, with a disposition to match.

Now, in September, Quinn's back with a story of his own. Set in the Wyoming wilderness, he learns a few things about women from snowbound beauty Amanda Callaway—and a lot more about love.

He's a Texan at heart...who soon has a Wyoming wedding in mind!

The Award of Excellence is given to one specially selected title per month. Spend September discovering *Sutton's Way* #670...only in Silhouette Romance.

RS670-1R

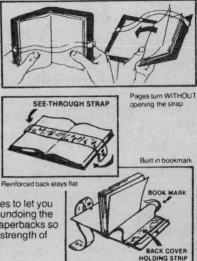